The
Diary Dilemma

An Ariel Hartman Mystery Based
on the Epistle of Galatians

The
Diary Dilemma

An Ariel Hartman Mystery Based
on the Epistle of Galatians

Jonathan M. George

The Diary Dilemma
An Ariel Hartman Mystery Based on the Epistle of Galatians

By Jonathan M. George

Cover design and interior layout by Laura Jurek

All Scriptures taken from the King James Version.
This novel is a work of fiction. All characters are fictional and any similarity to people living or dead is purely coincidential.

Printed in United States of America

WORD AFLAME PRESS
8855 Dunn Road, Hazelwood, MO 63042
www.pentecostalpublishing.com

Library of Congress Cataloging-in-Publication Data

George, Jonathan M., 1969-
   The diary dilemma : an Ariel Hartman mystery based on the Epistle of Galatians / by Jonathan M. George.
      p. cm.
   ISBN 978-1-56722-863-2 (alk. paper)
   I. Title.
   PZ7.G29332Di 2011
   [Fic]--dc23
                    2011028206

To my children:
Alyssa, Kayla, Darren, and Clayton.
Your dad loves you!

Preface

Some of the most powerful books of the Bible were written by Paul. But let's face it, Paul's writings are so profound and rich that many find them a mystery. That got me to thinking one day about how to explain some of his books (known as epistles) to kids. The answer was a mystery itself. That is, a kid's whodunit that weaves into the plot the major points Paul addressed in his epistles. But how will the reader recognize these points? The answer comes after the case has been solved and the bad guys are put away in "Ariel's After 'Word'" section, which guides the reader, as a detective, in his or her own investigation, searching for similarities between the story and the epistle. A little reading of the Bible is required. But not to worry, this section makes it easy.

Spoiler Alert!

"Ariel's After 'Word'" tells what happened in the story. Save it for last. No cheating!

So, grab a comfy chair or plop on your cushy couch, keep your Bible nearby, and enjoy a tale of intrigue and suspense as Ariel Hartman, the junior super-sleuth, outsmarts the criminals and leads you on a journey to understand God's Word.

Table of Contents

Prologue 11

Chapter 1   The Theft 13

Chapter 2   The Witness 17

Chapter 3   An Interview with the Curator 21

Chapter 4   The Thread 29

Chapter 5   The Assignment 33

Chapter 6   Secrets 39

Chapter 7   The Professor 43

Chapter 8   The Bookstore Proprietor 51

Chapter 9   The Graveyard 57

Chapter 10 The Buried Trunk 63

Chapter 11 Caught 67

Chapter 12 Shiny Green Things 71

Chapter 13 Back to the Beginning 77

Chapter 14 The Ignored Warning 83

Chapter 15 Family Ties 87

Chapter 16 The Search for Ariel 89

Chapter 17 Locked up! 93

Chapter 18 Breakthroughs and Setbacks 95

Chapter 19 Catch and Release 99

Chapter 20 Revelations 103

Chapter 21 The Cave 109

Chapter 22 Too Close for Comfort 113

Chapter 23 Can't Judge a Book by Its Cover 119

Epilogue 125

Ariel's After "Word" 127

Prologue

The man eased from his crouched position where he had hidden behind the stacks of boxes and picture frames tucked into the far corner of the dusty storage room. He crept to the door and pressed his ear against its cold metal frame. The only sound he heard was the hum of the air conditioner and the rhythmic beat of his heart. Satisfied that the coast was clear, the man clad in black pulled open the door and slipped out.

He slinked from room to room ducking behind poles, displays, plants, and just about anything the museum offered that could conceal his movements. Behind the mannequin dressed in the bright red uniform of a British officer from the American Revolution, the dark figure slid to the floor. He poked his head around the mannequin and eyed his prize just twenty feet away. But he would have to make a dash in front of the curator's office without being observed. On his knees, the man crawled to the edge of the wall and peered down the hallway to find the office door closed. He breathed a sigh of relief and then rose to his feet. The unwelcomed visitor tiptoed to the display case that held the book he came to reclaim.

Reaching into his pocket, he pulled out a pair of gloves and slid them expertly over his nimble fingers. With a gentle tug, the lid to the case opened with ease. He could not help but smile at his own cleverness. With the stealth of a cat, the thief snatched the book from its display stand and spun on his heels.

The bandit quickly retraced his steps to the storage room and exited into the alley between the museum and the library. The cool night air hit his face and flooded him with a rush of freedom. An ominous chuckle escaped his lips. From the nearby parking lot, he heard a car door slam. So he tucked the object of his evil deed under his arm and slithered into the shadows as he hurried down the alley. Convinced he had escaped unseen, he whistled a happy tune as he disappeared into the dark night.

The Theft

Ariel bent over the *Summerville Times* spread across the kitchen table. It wasn't much of a newspaper. After all, Summerville was a small town. But Ariel faithfully perused the paper every chance she got in search of a new mystery—some unsolved crime or lost pet, anything that would stimulate her detective inner ego—much to the consternation of her older brother Lenny.

"Could you please get the city news out of my bowl of corn flakes?" Lenny spewed small chunks of cereal and milk onto the headlines.

Ariel rolled her eyes while she snatched the bothersome and now soggy paper. "Can you be more disgusting? Ugh!"

Lenny replied with an I-don't-care shrug.

Ariel tossed the paper onto the kitchen counter. While she dabbed the pages with a napkin, an article caught her attention. "Wait! It says here there was a theft at the museum a couple of nights ago. Looks like some diary was stolen."

Again, Lenny gave her an I-don't-care shrug.

She ignored Lenny's insensitive attitude, or at least his transparent attempt at being insensitive. Ariel knew that he enjoyed going with her on what she called "cases." After he turned thirteen, though, he had to at least appear like such things were uncool. But Lenny still went, now on the excuse that he had to protect his baby sister. Ariel didn't mind. She liked having him around, even if he could be a pest.

Ariel leaned her long, slender frame across the counter and continued to read. "It goes on to say that the diary was written by one of the founders of Summerville who served as a soldier in the American Revolution. It was on loan to the museum by an owner who wished to remain anonymous."

"Oh, no!" Lenny pointed his finger at his sister. "You've got that look in your eyes. You're going to snoop around and try to solve this aren't you? Come on. It's Spring Break. Besides, have you already forgotten how hard Detective Sloan came down on you the last time you got all up in the cops' business?"

"I'll admit I almost got myself killed when I got trapped in that warehouse." Ariel tapped her head and gave Lenny a slight smile. "But, if it wasn't for my quick thinking, Detective Sloan would still be chasing that band of counterfeiters."

It was Lenny's turn to roll his eyes, and they both started chuckling. Their laughter was cut short by the door bell.

"I wonder who that could be," Ariel said. She hurried toward the front door.

Ariel came into the foyer just as her mother reached for the door knob. She stood on her tippy-toes and peered over her Mom's shoulder to get a look at their visitor.

What's Chelsea Jenkins doing here?

Sure, Ariel knew Chelsea from school. They were in the same classes after all. But Chelsea's popularity put her with a different set of friends. While Chelsea played the role of the prettiest girl in school, Ariel concerned herself with being the smartest. So, it surprised Ariel to see Chelsea standing on her doorstep.

"May I help you?" Ariel's Mom said politely.

"I'm here to see Ariel," Chelsea said.

14

"Over here." Ariel waved from behind her mother who moved aside to let Chelsea in. "This is a surprise. What brings you here?"

Chelsea gave an awkward glance toward Ariel's Mom who picked up the subtle hint, excusing herself from the room to give the girls their privacy.

"I hope that I didn't upset your mother. I've got a major secret, and I'm just kinda not sure who to tell right now. I know you can help me," Chelsea said.

Ariel shrugged. "She didn't seem upset to me. Come into the living room and let's talk about this secret of yours." Ariel led Chelsea out of the foyer and motioned for her to have a seat on the couch. Ariel sat in her father's worn-out recliner. "So, what's up?"

Chelsea twisted in her seat. "Did you hear about the theft at the museum?"

"Yeah, I just read about it in this morning's paper. Boy, I'd sure like to solve that case. What about it?"

"I might be able to help you out there. I'm pretty sure I saw who did it."

The Witness

The air around Ariel seemed to electrify. Just the thought of being the one to solve what probably was the most important case for the city of Summerville since ... well, Ariel couldn't think of a more important case. So lost in thought was she that she didn't hear Chelsea call her name.

"Ariel?" Chelsea waved her hand back and forth in the air to get Ariel's attention. "Earth to Ariel. Come in Ariel."

Ariel shook the dazed look from her face. "Oh, sorry. I guess I got a little lost in my thoughts there. Tell me everything. Don't leave any thing out."

"Tell you what?" Lenny appeared, leaning against the living room entry way. He gave Ariel a questioning look.

"Oh, hi, Lenny. This is Chelsea Jenkins," Ariel gestured. "She thinks she may have seen the thief who stole the diary from the museum." She turned to Chelsea, "You don't mind if my brother listens in, do you? He and I work together on a lot of cases."

Chelsea shook her head. "I don't mind. But I'm not exactly sure what I saw. I mean I'm pretty sure, but I'm not 100 percent positive."

"Just tell us what you think you saw, and we'll figure it out from there," Ariel said.

Chelsea took a deep breath. "My Mom and I went to the library two nights ago to get a book for my science project. You know, that project that's due in a couple of weeks?"

Ariel nodded. She had already finished the assignment days ago. Of course, Ariel usually finished most of her school projects early.

"It was around closing time," Chelsea continued. "I know, because I remember the librarian made an announcement that the library was closing in ten minutes. Mom and I took the books up to the front and waited for this old lady to slowly check us out. By the time we walked out, it was after nine o'clock. When we got to the car, that's when I saw him—the thief, I mean."

"Can you describe him?" Ariel asked.

"He was standing in the alley next to the museum. He had on a long raincoat and was wearing a hat pulled down low. It was hard to see his face, but there was just enough light to tell that he wore these really big glasses." Chelsea formed circles around her eyes with her fingers to give the impression of eyeglasses. "He was carrying some book. As soon as he saw me, he shoved the book under his arm and ran off down the alley."

Ariel heard the quake in Chelsea's voice. She walked over and sat next to Chelsea. "You must have been scared. Did your Mom see the guy?"

Chelsea slowly shook her head. "She was too busy looking for her keys. By the time she found them and got in the car, the guy was gone."

"Did you tell her what you saw?"

"No, because I thought he was just some creep hanging out by the museum. I didn't know about the robbery then."

Lenny noisily dropped into the recliner that Ariel had vacated. He began to twirl the chair from side to side. The unexpected commotion made Ariel cringe. He can't pay attention for more than a minute. But she pretended to ignore the distraction.

"Okay, so what makes you so sure he was the thief and not just some creep hanging around?"

Chelsea stared at Ariel with a look of shock. "Because of the newspaper! This morning when I came down for breakfast, my dad read about a thief that stole a diary. It had to be the diary the guy was carrying. It scared me so bad that I came so close to this robber that I dropped a pitcher of orange juice all over the floor."

"Surely you told them about the guy then, didn't you?" Ariel said.

Chelsea covered her face with her hands. "No. I didn't know what to do." After a couple of seconds, she lowered her hands and looked up at Ariel, tears forming in her eyes. "I was afraid they'd start worrying over nothing. But the more I thought about it, the more scared I got. What if this guy really did get a good look at me? Then I thought about you, Ariel. You would know what to do."

Ariel grabbed a strand of her waist-length auburn hair and rolled the ends around her finger. Her sapphire eyes gazed intensely into the distance. She wasn't looking at anything in particular, nor was she primping her hair. This was just a habit she did often when deep in thought.

Several tense moments ticked away as she considered her response. Finally, she turned to Chelsea. "Your mom's a lawyer right?"

"Yes, but I'm not sure how that—"

Ariel raised her hand to stop Chelsea. "I think you need to tell her, and I think you need to get down to the police station and talk to Detective Sloan. Make a statement, but get your mom to put some heat on the cops to keep an eye on you for a couple of days. I doubt the guy got as good a look at you as you did of him. He was standing under the light, but you were in the dark mostly because that parking lot at the library is not well lit. But better to be safe."

"Will you come with me to the police station?"

Ariel grimaced. "I'm not sure that's such a good idea. Let's just say that Detective Sloan finds me—oh, what's the word?"

"*Irritating*," Lenny said.

Ariel reached for a couch pillow to throw at Lenny. While he peeled the pillow from his face, Ariel turned back to Chelsea. "Besides, I think my comedian brother over here and I would do much better going to the museum to ask a few questions."

An Interview with the Curator

When Ariel and Lenny arrived at the museum later that morning, they caught the curator just leaving to grab a snack. They stood in the sparse museum lobby where old photographs from the 1940s lined the walls, portraying the construction of the museum and the way the town's market square looked back then. A long oak registration counter took up most of the space in the lobby where a woman with deep wrinkles and curly coral blue hair sat flipping through a magazine. Mrs. Carmichael leaned against the counter, her black leather billfold cradled in her pudgy hands.

"Horrible! Just horrible! And in our little town! Who would do such a thing?" Mrs. Penelope Carmichael's cheeks burned bright red on her wizened plump face. She peered over her horn-rimmed glasses at Ariel and Lenny; despair filled her soft gray eyes. Ariel, concerned that Mrs. Carmichael might have a stroke, began to question her with great care. "I don't know who would do such a thing either," she said softly, "but I hope they catch him soon."

"Would you mind telling us more about the diary theft, Mrs. Carmichael?" Ariel asked.

"Well, it was about ten o'clock. We had been closed for an hour. I usually stay a little later to do some paperwork in my office. It's so much quieter then, I suppose. Anyway, as I was leaving to go home, I happened to pass the diary display and saw the case lid opened. I looked inside, but the diary was gone. I searched all around but could not find it. I could have sworn the diary was there when we locked up at nine o'clock. I tell you, this whole thing is a travesty and an embarrassment!"

The timeline seemed to fit with when Chelsea saw the mysterious man emerge from the alleyway. Still, Ariel could not rule out an inside job. "Do you have a security man that locks up for you?"

Mrs. Carmichael's breathing relaxed and her cheeks returned to their normal pallor. "I did about a year ago, but when money got tight with budget cuts … well … I had to let him go."

"Do you think he might have had anything to do with this? You know, out of revenge for losing his job."

Mrs. Carmichael threw her head back and laughed. "Oh, my, no! Not our dear Henry. Oh heavens no! He was nearly eighty when I let him go, and he so looked forward to it. He called it 'his retirement.' Soon after, Henry moved to Florida to live with his ailing sister. Last I heard, she passed away and he was living in a nursing home outside of Boca Raton."

"Do you have any idea why someone would want to steal the diary?" Ariel said.

"My goodness, you are an inquisitive child." Mrs. Carmichael pushed her glasses further up the bridge of her nose. "But didn't you say you had a friend who may have seen the thief?"

Ariel hesitated. She didn't want to get Mrs. Carmichael's hopes up. Chelsea's description of the man was pretty sketchy. "Umm, it's possible she did, but she's not too sure. It was pretty dark."

"I see," Mrs. Carmichael said despondently. "To answer your question why someone would steal the diary, it might be best if I show you."

Mrs. Carmichael tucked her billfold under the eave of the registration desk. To the ancient woman sitting behind the desk, she said, "Madge, will you hold this for me while I show these children to my office?"

Madge just looked up and smiled, flashing teeth too pearly to be real for her age. Ariel suspected they were dentures.

"Follow me," Mrs. Carmichael wagged her finger to Ariel and Lenny. The plump museum caretaker lumbered down the main corridor of the museum, which opened into an expansive rotunda area. The two young detectives admired the marble flooring and carved mahogany patterned after ancient Grecian architecture. At the center of the room a glassed directory displayed a map of the museum and the location of specific artifacts. Mrs. Carmichael moved past it toward a room filled with American Revolutionary memorabilia.

Lenny stopped in front of the directory and began to read. Ariel, after realizing that Lenny was not beside her, spun around. "Psst, Lenny," she whispered. "You coming, or what?"

"Oops. Sorry, just looking." He jogged over to Ariel.

Luckily, Mrs. Carmichael moved rather slowly. Ariel and Lenny had no trouble catching up. She took them into the middle of the American Revolution room where she gestured to a display case cordoned off by a red velvet rope. "The diary was displayed over there, but you can't touch it. The police told me that I am to keep everyone away."

Mrs. Carmichael continued down the next hallway and stopped at a door with a sign that read CURATOR. She tugged at the chain around her neck that held a set of keys. "Be careful," she said, twisting the key into the lock and pushing the door open. "My office's in a bit of disarray. I need to do some filing but haven't had the time."

Inside the cluttered office, stacks of books rose several feet into the air like miniature high-rise buildings. Mountains of bulging manila folders rested at odd angles against the end of a filing cabinet tucked into the corner of the office. Ariel thought that if someone sneezed hard enough, whole stacks would come crashing down. She fought her compulsion to organize the mess.

Mrs. Carmichael went behind her desk and moved several heaps of papers to make a small clearing. She sat down and began shuffling through one of the many piles of folders.

"Ah, here they are." She pulled out a thick stack of photographs held together by a large binder clip. She walked them over to where Ariel and Lenny stood by the door. They had to stand because books and folders filled the chairs in front of the desk, leaving no place to sit. "These are the photographs of the diary." She showed the first picture. "Here is the outside of the diary. It's handcrafted in leather with gold leaf fringed designs around the corners. Judging by the time and materials it would have taken to make such a book suggests this diary was intended to be a keepsake."

Mrs. Carmichael flipped to the second photograph and explained. "The author dedicated the diary to someone named Barney."

"Who's Barney?" Ariel said.

"I'm not sure. It was probably a family member or a loved one."

At the third photograph she paused. "Here's why I wanted to show you these photographs. This is probably the reason the thief took the diary." She pointed to a place on the picture. "Do you recognize whose signature this is on the margin of the page?"

Ariel and Lenny craned their necks for a closer look. "Looks like George Washington," blurted Lenny.

"That's correct," Mrs. Carmichael said.

"But who are these other people?" Ariel tapped on the other names written on the page.

"We're not sure. We believe they're other soldiers. Can you see what's written above their signatures?"

Ariel squinted to make out the details. "It looks like, 'To Freedom and Country,'" she said.

"That's correct. We believe that it was a little statement to help rally the troops to keep on fighting." Mrs. Carmichael pumped her arm in the air in a gesture of victory.

"How do you know these signatures are real, especially George Washington's?"

"When we received the diary, I had our town's local used book dealer, Nate Porter, look at it. He's certified to make these kinds of appraisals. He confirmed that they were, in fact, real."

"Can we see the other photographs, Mrs. Carmichael?" Ariel said.

The next photograph Mrs. Carmichael showed was of a crude hand-drawn map. "This is believed to be a layout of the Battle of Trenton." She traced a penciled line at the bottom of the picture. "Down here is the Delaware River, I believe, that Washington and the soldiers crossed to the battle."

The other photographs were of the other pages in the diary. There was a photograph for every page.

Lenny shook his head. "Its cool how well kept this diary was. It doesn't look all beaten up like other stuff from that long ago."

"That's true, young man. Wherever this diary was kept, it was handled with a great deal of care." Mrs. Carmichael replaced the binder clip and returned the pictures to the folder.

"The newspaper said the owner did not want to be named. I assume you know, right?" Ariel asked.

"I'm afraid I do not," Mrs. Carmichael said, shaking her head. "You see, about three weeks ago I got this letter from an attorney in Raleigh about this diary had that had been in his client's family for generations. The letter explained that it had been written by a founder of Summerville who fought in the war for independence. His client wanted to know if I'd be interested in showcasing it here so that arrangements could be made to have it sent. But his client wanted to remain anonymous."

"Boy, I bet his client was mad when he learned about the theft," Lenny said.

"That's just the thing. We've tried, as have the police, in reaching the attorney to share the bad news, but his number's been disconnected. Calls to directory assistance and online searches have yielded nothing either. It's like he just disappeared."

"That is odd," Ariel commented.

"Yes it is," Mrs. Carmichael said. "And I was about to spend a great deal of money on advertisement to draw people to the exhibit. I guess I dodged a bullet there."

"Well, thank you, Mrs. Carmichael. You've been very kind to talk to us and show us the pictures. I'm sure the diary and the owner will show up soon." Ariel glanced around the room. "By the way, if you ever need anybody to help you organize your office, I'd be happy to volunteer."

As Ariel and Lenny left, Mrs. Carmichael scanned her disheveled office. "Hmmm," she mumbled. "Yes, yes, I suppose I really do need to pick up around here."

Outside her office, Ariel grabbed Lenny's hand and pulled him down the hallway.

"Hey, ease up, Sis. I can walk, you know," he said.

"We need to hurry before she comes back out," Ariel said.

"Hurry for what?"

Ariel stopped in front of the diary display case. She leaned into Lenny's ear. "I want you to stand outside the room and make sure no one sees me. I'm going to check out this case."

"Are you crazy?" Lenny said in a forced whisper. "Detective Sloan told Mrs. Carmichael to have everyone stay clear of this case. What if you get caught?"

"No, he said not to have anybody *touch* the case. I will not touch it, I promise. And, I won't get caught if you do your job as lookout." She shoved Lenny toward the room entrance. "Now go."

Lenny reluctantly went, mumbling under his breath.

Ariel heard some comment about her sanity, or her lack thereof, and how he wished he would have stayed home to play "Autoban Racer" on his video game player. She paid no attention to his whiney rant. Instead, she set to work to investigate the display.

First, she walked the perimeter of the velvet rope, standing on her toes to peer inside the empty case. Next, she scanned the outside of the case. The police had brushed it for prints, leaving a hint of chalky blue residue behind. Her focus turned to the lock where she looked for any evidence of tool marks. Did the thief pick his way into the case? Not finding any marks, she knelt down and looked underneath the case. Except for dusty, spider-webbed paneling, she didn't see any forced entry.

Bewildered by the lack of clues, Ariel absentmindedly pulled herself up by a metal pole that held one end of the velvet rope. She didn't realize how unstable it was until far too late. The pole pitched to the right. The rope tugged on the opposite pole which gave way and tumbled to the floor with a loud clatter. Ariel lost her balance and rolled face up on top of the heap.

That was when Ariel saw the black thread wedged into the bottom edge of the display case.

4

The Thread

Ariel grabbed the thread and tucked it into her pocket. She had just rolled onto her side when she saw Lenny charging toward her.

Lenny took her by the hand, pulling her to her feet. "What happened?"

"I lost my balance when I tried to stand up, I guess." She brushed the dust from her skirt.

Mrs. Carmichael rounded the corner, her hands on her hips. "Just what in the world do you two think you're doing?" The curator shook her finger precariously close to the end of Ariel's nose. "I thought I told you to stay away from this display." Mrs. Carmichael stared at the floor. "Now just look at this mess."

"I'm truly sorry, Mrs. Carmichael." Ariel stepped behind Lenny for safe cover. "I promise I did not touch the case. But, I'll admit I did look around. I must have grabbed the wrong end of the pole."

Mrs. Carmichael sighed. "Were you hurt?"

Ariel shook her head. "I don't think so. Again, I'm sorry for all this trouble, but I had to see for myself just how the thief got into the case." She pointed to the lock. "Mrs. Carmichael, do you find any tool marks on the display lock?"

"I'm not sure I understand what you mean."

"If there are no tool marks to show the lock was picked, how else could the thief have gotten in—unless the case was unlocked or they had the key?"

Mrs. Carmichael raised an eyebrow. "I can assure you it was locked, and I'm the only one with the key."

"Do you mind if I ask you when it was last opened?"

"On the day of the crime, I opened the case twice—once for Mr. Porter and again for a board member. The lid automatically latches when it's closed, and since I closed the lid, I'm sure that it relocked. All I can say is that it must have been a very clever bandit that made off with the diary." Mrs. Carmichael gestured to the pile of rope and fallen poles. "Now if you two will help me set this rope right, I will very much appreciate it."

Ariel stood one of the poles upright and tightly screwed it back to its base. Lenny grabbed the other pole and then re-anchored the velvet rope to each end.

"Thank you both," Mrs. Carmichael said. "Now, I believe its time for you to leave."

Ariel made her final apologies. As she left the room, she glanced over her shoulder at Mrs. Carmichael who bent down and stared into the lock. "She's going to go blind looking at that lock trying to figure out how someone got in there."

Lenny stole a look toward the perplexed curator. "So how do you think they got in?"

"I don't know but they sure didn't pick their way in, that's for sure. But that's not all I found." She dug into her pocket and pulled out a fuzzy piece of black thread, handing it to Lenny. "Look at this little clue."

He turned it over between his fingers. "So when does dryer lint become a clue?"

"Its not dryer lint, doofus," retorted Ariel. "It's a thread from a glove. I found it stuck in the corner of the case."

"How are you so sure this came from a glove?" Lenny said. "This could have come from anything. Someone could have snagged their sweater on the edge of the case for all we know."

Ariel snatched the thread out of his hand. "Look closer," she said, holding it near Lenny's face. "Doesn't this look like it came from one of those cheap dollar-store cloth gloves?"

Lenny shrugged. "Looks like lint to me."

Ariel jabbed the thread back into her skirt pocket. "It's from a glove, and I bet it's from the thief." She huffed toward the main corridor with Lenny on her tail.

"No need to get all testy, Ariel," Lenny said. "If you say it's from a glove, it's from a glove."

Ariel kept walking. She charged right past the registration desk and pushed through the door.

Lenny nodded nervously to the elderly Madge behind the desk whose eyes looked up from her magazine to watch Ariel's grand exit from the museum.

Ariel's anger quickly turned to shock when she did not spot their bikes out front.

"Hey, where's our bikes?" Lenny said. He threw his hands in the air. "Well, that's just great! First someone steals a dumb old diary. Now they jack our bikes. What's gotten into this one-horse town?"

From behind them a shadow moved across the lawn, blocking out the sun. Ariel gasped when she noticed the distinct outline of a holstered pistol.

"I took your bikes," a gruff voice called out.

Ariel's Assignment

Ariel and Lenny turned slowly, their eyes wide as saucers. A hulk of a man stepped toward them, his folded arms tugged at the taut fabric of his sleeve.

"Detective Sloan! What brings you here?" Ariel forced an awkward smile. His presence brought her both a level of comfort and dread. The detective was an imposing man who resembled more a wrestler than a small-town law officer. She was glad he was one of the good guys, although she had a feeling he wasn't here for a friendly visit.

"I'd much rather know why you took our bikes," Lenny grumbled.

Detective Sloan raised his hands, palms up. "Relax kids. Chelsea came by the station and gave me her statement, but a little fact slipped out." He stared directly at Ariel. "She told me that you were going to see Mrs. Carmichael. After the last time you tried to help out with a case, I thought the least I could do was check on you. And since I'm here, I thought I'd offer you a ride home." The police officer pointed to the trunk of his car. "See? I've got your bikes locked up safe and sound."

Ariel stared dumbfounded at her bike bolted to the back of a patrol car. She tried to absorb the barrage of questions that filled her head. Did Chelsea snitch on her? Not that she was doing anything bad, but after Ariel told her how the detective felt about her, it didn't make sense. And how much should she tell Detective Sloan? He would not be too pleased with the little mishap earlier at the display case. Maybe she could sweet-talk her way out of this.

"Thanks for the offer, Detective Sloan." Ariel flashed her best smile. "No need to go out of your way. I'm sure you've got more important things to do. We can ride ourselves home."

"Ah, it's no problem at all." The burley detective waved them to follow. He stared at Ariel over the top of his sunglasses. "Besides, I get the impression you're snooping into this stolen diary case. I think a quiet drive and a little talk would be just the thing, don't you?"

Ariel felt her stomach drop to her knees.

Lenny just shrugged. "Do we have a choice?"

Detective Sloan reached his car. "Not really." He yanked the handle to the back door of his squad car and nodded for them to get in. Ariel and Lenny gave each other an anxious look and then scooted into the back seat. Detective Sloan gave them a wink before closing the door.

Lenny leaned toward Ariel. "Are we being arrested?"

"I don't think so. But, he's going to try to find out what we know." She chewed a fingernail nervously watching Detective Sloan speak into the walkie-talkie strapped to his shoulder. "Since we're trapped like rats, we might as well use this to our advantage and find out what he knows too."

"Okay, but what do we know?"

Ariel did not have time to respond before Detective Sloan slid behind the steering wheel. After giving them a quick glance in the rearview mirror, he started the car and eased out of the parking lot.

"So, I guess you two either didn't get my message the last time we had this problem, or you ignored it. But I want you to stay away from police business. It's not like looking for someone's lost cat or misplaced necklace. This is a crime. If whoever did this was desperate enough to steal the diary right under Mrs. Carmichael's nose, you can be sure he's desperate enough to get rid of a couple of nosy kids who get in his way."

"So, you know it was a man then?" Ariel felt her courage begin to return.

"A man?" Detective Sloan gave Ariel another quick glance in the rearview mirror. "What are you talking about?"

"You said 'he,' so obviously you know it was a man."

"You're putting words in my mouth. I said 'he' as a figure of speech. We don't know who did this—man, woman or gang for that matter."

"Well, what do you think? Could it have been a professional hit?"

The detective shifted uneasily in his seat. "There's a good chance it may be. The robber got into that case without leaving so much as a mark or a fingerprint. But, I'm the one to ask the questions here. Not you. So, let's find out what you know there, Ms. Mystery Girl."

Lenny snickered at Detective Sloan's jibe. Ariel gritted her teeth and gave Lenny a good punch in the leg. "Ow," Lenny yelped.

"I guess I know as much as you do," Ariel said. "Chelsea gave me a description of the thief, which I told her to give to you. Mrs. Carmichael gave us a history lesson about the diary, and we got a chance to look at the diary case. That's about it. All except for a piece of black thread I saw caught in the case."

"Thread? What thread?" the detective asked a little too harshly.

Ariel retrieved the thread and gave it to Detective Sloan. "I know it could have come from anywhere but maybe you can have it analyzed. I'm sure it's from a glove."

The detective shoved it into his shirt pocket. He pulled the car to the side of the road and then turned around in his seat to face Ariel. "Listen, I know you want to help. But you have a tendency of getting in over your head. I don't want you getting hurt." He sighed as he ran his hand through his hair. "Still, maybe you two can help me out. Secretly, of course, and under my strict directions."

Ariel looked at Lenny, but Lenny had his MP3 player ear buds jammed into his ears mouthing the words to some song. She shook her head and returned the detective's gaze. "What have you got in mind, officer?"

"Too many people shut down when a police officer comes around. They see the badge and think they're in trouble."

Ariel laughed as she looked at where she sat—in a squad car with a big officer in the front seat. "Yeah, I can see how that could happen."

Detective Sloan followed her eyes and laughed too. "I guess I've proven my point. Anyway, maybe with you they'd be less guarded. Also, I'm not very good with a computer. Why don't you and your brother there do a little digging for me into how much a diary like this might be worth? Do a little Internet research. Talk to your Dad. Maybe he knows another professor at the university where he works who is an expert in this kind of stuff. I'll leave the research to you. You leave tracking down the thief to me. Deal?"

Ariel realized this would be a perfect arrangement. She could find out more about the value, which she was going to do anyway, but now she had the backing of the police—to some extent. It was an offer she could not refuse. "You got yourself a deal." Ariel stuck out her hand for Detective Sloan to shake.

"Great!" Detective Sloan shook her hand. He pulled down his car's sun visor, took out a business card, and handed it to Ariel. "My email address is on there. When you find something, drop me a line. Now, if you will excuse me, this is where I let you off. Can't have your parents worried by having a cop drive you home, can we?" He hopped out and walked to the back of the car.

Ariel turned to Lenny and yanked out his earpieces.

"Ouch, what's that for?" he yelled.

"This is where we get off, genius."

Lenny looked out the window. "But I thought he was taking us home."

"Too early for that. We've got work to do."

The detective unhooked the bikes from the rack and set them on their kickstands on the sidewalk near the edge of the road. He then opened Ariel's door. But as she began to get out, he motioned her to wait. "Listen, Ariel. I meant what I said. This could get dangerous. Don't go being a hero."

She nudged him aside and stepped out of the car. Turning back to the detective, she said, "I will be careful. Besides, God always looks out for me."

"I know you believe that, but don't go tempting Him either. Okay?"

Ariel nodded and waved Lenny to follow.

Outside, Lenny asked, "So, what's this work we have to do, little sis?"

She did not answer.

"Hello?" Lenny said sarcastically.

Ariel shook her head and started peddling. "If you'd pay attention, you'd know Detective Sloan asked for our help. So hurry up!"

"Ugh!" Lenny jumped on his bike and caught up to Ariel, still clueless where they were headed.

Secrets

The warm afternoon sun bore down upon Ariel and her brother as they zoomed along sidewalks and streets. Ariel found the occasional breeze inviting to her flushed cheeks. The ride gave her time to plan how she and Lenny would research the diary's value. And like all her plans that included Lenny, she kept him completely in the dark until time to put her plan into action. Lenny didn't seem to mind. He raced behind Ariel, his ear buds planted firmly in his ears, drumming on his handlebars.

They soon arrived at the library. Ariel glanced at the museum next door and shuddered as she thought about the dark figure Chelsea saw lurking in the alleyway just a few short nights before. Once just a forgotten relic of days gone by, the museum now seemed to take on an evil presence. Ariel shook off the impression while she and Lenny parked their bikes near the library's entrance.

The glass door slid open to a world of books that filled the long lines of shelves. Ariel brightened as she breathed in the fragrance of thousands of pages of knowledge. *No other smell on earth like a book.*

The librarian didn't even bother to lift her nose out of her romance novel when Ariel and Lenny passed by the collections booth. Ariel hurried Lenny to the bank of computers at the center of the library where she grabbed a clipboard next to the computers and quickly jotted their names on the log sheet.

"Lenny, you take Computer 10, and I'll take Computer 11," Ariel said.

Lenny strolled to the computer with a big "10" taped to its monitor. He dropped into the seat and eyed Ariel. "Should I be looking for recipes? Or better yet, how to read the minds of crazy girls who like to solve mysteries?"

Ariel laughed. Maybe she should have at least told him a part of her plan. "Oh, sorry. Detective Sloan wants us to figure out how much the diary might be worth. Check out any online auctions you can find. See if there's anything that might be similar to the diary and what people are bidding on it these days. Look especially for any journals written by a soldier from the American Revolution or something signed by George Washington."

Lenny watched Ariel type in an access number. One more thing Ariel forgot to tell him. He scooted his chair down the bank of computers and stretched for the clipboard. After making a mental note of the code, he rolled back and typed in the digits. As he waited for the computer to pull up the Internet browser, he leaned toward Ariel. "And may I ask what you're going to be looking for?"

"I'm going to search museums to see if they've ever exhibited a diary like this one or, hopefully, even this particular diary. Then I'm going to dig around a bunch of antiquarian book dealer websites."

Lenny raised an eyebrow. "Antiquarian? You're going to look for books on fish?"

"*Antiquarian*, not aquarium, goofball. Like antiques—antiquarian. Get it? I'm looking for places that sell really old books."

"Well, why didn't you just say that? Antiquarian. Phft."

Ariel rolled her eyes and wondered how her brother could be such an airhead and yet be the family's math whiz. He had a knack for numbers without even trying while she studied her brains out for the grades she made. She had to stop herself before she got too riled up.

Focus, Ariel. Focus.

Focus she did, but all for naught. After an hour and a half of mouse-clicking and Web browsing, they came up with zilch. Ariel slumped in her seat. "Nothing. I found absolutely nothing." She turned to Lenny. "What about you?"

Lenny fell back in his seat and sighed. "Not much really. I found several auctions where stuff signed by Washington was going for about $1,000 to $2,000."

"Yeah, I also found a website that sells old and rare books. There was a book signed by Washington going for about five grand. Nothing about a diary written by a soldier, though. And absolutely no information on any museum sites I found." Ariel dropped her head onto the table with a soft thud and let out a sad moan. "What are we going to do now?" She rolled her head toward Lenny. "What's so special about this dumb diary anyway?"

Lenny shrugged. "Beats me, but I don't think ole Georgie's signature had much to do with it. Something must be pretty important about this diary though. I don't know what it is. But there is one thing for sure. If I don't leave soon and find a snack or something, I'm going to eat my shoe. Can we go now?"

"Yeah, I guess there's nothing more to do here." Ariel logged off the computer and scooted her chair underneath the table. She and Lenny passed unnoticed by the librarian who was still engrossed in her book.

"You know what gets me about this whole diary business?" Lenny stepped on the sensor to the automatic sliding glass door.

"What's that?"

"To find out some dude even wrote a diary."

Ariel's forehead wrinkled. "I don't get what you mean."

"Think about it. The only people I know who write in diaries are girls, and only their deepest, darkest secrets."

Ariel grabbed the handlebars to her bike and pulled it to the sidewalk. "Times were different back then, but ...." She froze. Something about what Lenny said intrigued her. Secrets. She stared mesmerized into the alley between the library and museum where Chelsea had seen the sinister man on the night of the crime.

"Ariel, you okay?" Lenny waved a hand in front of Ariel's face. "Looks like you've seen a ghost."

She ignored him. Instead she cast her eyes toward the horizon as the sun dropped lower from the sky, soon to shroud the town in a cover of darkness. Ariel considered what secrets might be shrouded in the pages of the stolen diary.

Lost in thought, Ariel did not hear the man approach. But she sure felt his large hand pressing its long fingers into her thin shoulder.

The Professor

"Whoa! Ariel, it's just me!"

"Dad!" Ariel flung her arms around her father's waist and buried her face into his chest. "You scared me."

Dr. Hartman returned his daughter's embrace and kissed the top of her head. Ariel gazed up into her father's deep blue eyes. No doubt she got her eyes from him. His short-cropped salt-and-pepper hair and the reading glasses resting on the end of his nose gave him that distinguished look of a college professor.

"Yo, Dad. What's up?" Lenny gave his father a cool-guy nod.

Dr. Hartman returned his son's greeting with a light punch on the arm. "Hey, kid," he said. "What are you two doing here?"

"We're doing a little research," Ariel replied. "You know that diary that was stolen from the museum a few days ago?"

"I read something about it." Dr. Hartman paused. "Are you snooping around again, Ariel?"

"We're just looking online for information about how much the diary was worth. Detective Sloan asked us to. What about you? What are you doing here?"

"You remember Dr. Hunter? We're conducting an experiment and there are a couple of books from the library we need." He then reached into his pocket and took out a pen and scrap of paper. "Listen, I'm going to write down a name of a professor at the college that might be able to help you out in your research."

He handed the paper to Ariel. "Dr. Allen Smith," she read.

"Dr. Smith has a doctorate in history and happens to be a renowned expert on antiquities. He's written several papers on ancient history."

Ariel gave her father a puzzled look. "But, we're not talking ancient history. We're talking American history. Isn't that different?"

"Dr. Smith studies all kinds of history, including American. And his knowledge of antiquities may help explain what makes this old diary so valuable. It's worth a shot." Ariel's father raised a warning finger. "But, I don't want you getting in Dr. Smith's way. He's a busy man. And I don't want you getting into any more trouble with your investigations."

"I won't, Dad," Ariel said.

"Good. I need to get back to the lab soon, so let me get in there and get these books. You two get home soon before your mom worries. I'll see you at dinner." Dr. Hartman waved to his children and walked toward the library entrance.

Ariel turned to Lenny and grinned. Lenny shuddered. "I know that look, Ariel," he said. "You're going to drag me down to the college tomorrow, aren't you?"

Ariel gave Lenny that "Oh, yeah" nod.

"Great. And during Spring Break when I hoped to sleep late and veg out in front of my video games. Guess that won't be happening."

Even with a jacket, Ariel shivered at the cool wind that blew across her thin frame and shook the branches of the trees. She wrapped her arms around her chest and gazed at the dark cloud that hung in the morning sky. She turned to Lenny. "We need to get a move on. It's about to rain."

Lenny looked up. "Yep. Looks like a big storm's a-coming. How about we blow off this trip to see Dr. Smith and go inside for some hot chocolate and a game of 'Speed Demon 2'?"

"I don't think so," Ariel said, jumping on her bike. She peddled as fast as she could to race the approaching storm.

Lenny followed but struggled to keep up. After a mile, Lenny called out to Ariel. "You know ... you may wear skirts, Ariel, but you are more boy than girl," he said, huffing and puffing.

Ariel laughed. "You just don't like the fact that a girl can beat you." She pressed the peddles harder and pulled further away from Lenny.

Lenny shook his head. There was no way he could move that fast.

By the time they reached the university and found the bike rack, raindrops dotted the pavement. They locked up their bikes then raced toward the faculty building.

The university was built over one hundred years ago in classic-style red brick common in early American colonial times. About thirty years ago, two buildings were added to either side of the original construction to meet the demand for more classroom and faculty space. Thankfully for Ariel and Lenny, the faculty offices were located in the building closest to the student parking lot.

"Do you know where you're going?" Lenny said, jogging up the stairs.

"Dad said Dr. Smith's office is on the same floor as his, five rooms down. I just hope he's in."

As they stepped through the glassed entrance, smells of old books and cleaning solution filled their nostrils. The place seemed to demand reverence and quiet. Except for the sounds of Lenny's wet tennis shoes squeaking against the linoleum floor, Ariel and Lenny moved down the hall in complete silence.

They came upon Dr. Hartman's office and peered in, but the room was empty. They continued further down the hallway and counted off doors until they reached the one with the name D<small>R</small>. A<small>LLEN</small> S<small>MITH</small> etched in white letters on a black placard.

Ariel peeked through the small window of the door. "I don't see anyone in there," she said.

Lenny nudged Ariel aside. "Here, let me have a look." He pressed his face to the glass.

"May I help you?" said a snobbish voice from behind them.

Ariel and Lenny twirled around. "Um, we're looking for Dr. Smith." Ariel's voice cracked.

The man stared at them down his beak-like nose. "I am Dr. Smith, and who might you be? Certainly, you can't be students unless we started taking them younger these days."

"My name is Ariel Hartman, and this is my brother, Lenny. We're Dr. Hartman's kids." She pointed down the hall. "You know, the psychology professor."

"Ah, yes. I know Dr. Hartman very well. I understand he and Dr. Hunter are in the middle of some important experiments. Come into my office and tell me how I may be of service."

He opened the door and let them through. Dr. Smith's office was immaculate. A photograph of it could be taken for the front cover of an office supply catalog. Diplomas, accommodations, and certificates filled the walls. The bookshelf behind his desk held all sorts of scholarly books and trinkets from foreign countries. Dr. Smith slipped into his maroon leather chair behind the clutter-free mahogany desk. He motioned for the two to have a seat in the matching leather chairs in front of his enormous desk.

Ariel cleared her throat. "My dad suggested I come see you because you are an expert on history. Did you happen to hear about the theft the other night at the museum? Somebody took a diary written by a soldier from the Battle of Trenton."

Dr. Smith leaned back in his oversized chair. "Ah, yes. I do recall reading about that in the paper. Seemed to be hot news in our little community and a bit of an embarrassment to the museum. But I hardly see how I can be of any help."

"We were wondering what makes this diary so special," Ariel said.

"Hmm, well I can only speculate as I know very little about the diary in this case. But I have to assume that this diary is very rare. That alone doesn't necessarily make it valuable though. For that, it must hold some significant importance."

"Significant importance?" Ariel questioned.

"Yes. Let me explain." Dr. Smith propped his feet on his desk. "Let's say that you found a play written four hundred years ago among the rubble of someone's attic. It may be the only copy in the world. That makes it rare. But if it were written by an unknown author, it may not hold much value. Now if the play was written by, say, William Shakespeare, well, it could be worth quite a bit to some people."

"I think I understand, but I'm not sure how this fits in with why someone would steal an old diary?" Ariel said.

"I seem to recall it was a firsthand account by a soldier in a significant battle of the American Revolution. That's rare. It too has extraordinary value because it's signed by Washington, which I think I read. Add that to the fact that the diary's author is an original founder of Summerville and you start to paint a picture of its worth and importance, at least to our community."

"How much do you think a book like that is worth dollar-wise?" Lenny chimed in.

"It's hard to say what one would pay for that book. But considering its importance, I'd be inclined to say between $8,000 and $10,000."

"That's a lot of money, but is it worth the trouble to steal it?" Ariel asked.

Dr. Smith dropped his feet to the ground and folded his arms across his desk. Then with a soft laugh he said, "Well, you see, that depends on the desperation of the criminal. Or perhaps there is a value hidden that if most knew about, many might be more understanding of the thief's intent. Of course, that's just my guess."

Secrets, thought Ariel.

"Well, thank you for your time, Dr. Smith. I hope we didn't bother you too much," Ariel said.

"It was my pleasure," he said jovially. As they stood, Dr. Smith held up a hand. "Just out of curiosity, why are two kids so interested in some old book? It seems you'd be much more interested in something less prehistoric, like playing video games or texting friends."

Ariel grimaced at the comment. It never ceased to amaze her the number of adults that thought kids were nothing more than empty-headed, video-addicted nincompoops incapable of thought or reason. However, she let it pass—if for no other reason than she did not want to embarrass her father. "Well, Dr. Smith," she said instead, "we have a friend who may have witnessed the crime, so of course we are very interested. But I think we've taken up enough—"

"Wait," Dr. Smith interrupted Ariel. "Did you say you have a friend who may have witnessed the crime? Do the police know?"

"Yes sir, she has given a full report. But it was dark and she didn't get a very good look at him. Well, we better get going." Ariel rose from her chair. "Thank you for your time, Dr. Smith."

"Of course, children," Dr. Smith said through a cordial smile. "I do hope they find the fiend responsible for this. I am glad to help in any way I can. By the way, again just out of curiosity, what are you going to do next?"

"The museum curator said that she used a man named Nate Porter to check out the diary. He's supposed to be an expert in rare books and owns a bookstore in town. Maybe he can tell us a little more about the diary."

Dr. Smith frowned. "Nate Porter?! I find it very curious that he comes to town not more than two months ago and happens to be an "expert" on the very book that was stolen. You mark my words—he has something to do with this. I would not be surprised if he has criminal connections to get rid of a book like that ... for a hefty price, of course."

"Well, thanks again," Ariel said.

As soon as she and Lenny walked out of his office, Lenny whispered to Ariel, "He seems a little suspicious of that Porter dude, huh?"

"Just a bit," Ariel replied.

They headed down the hallway and pushed open the exit door. The rain had stopped and the sun shone brightly, casting shimmery reflections off the puddles on the pavement. The chilly air gave way to a humidity that enveloped Ariel. But it did little to suppress the chill she felt inside as she considered how cold the trail was leading to the diary's abductor.

Ariel rolled some strands of hair around her index finger. There were too many questions still rattling around that brain of hers. Is $8,000 really worth stealing a diary? What if the diary does hold some secrets more valuable than its apparent worth? What's Dr. Smith got against Mr. Porter? Where is the diary's owner, and, for that matter, where's Chelsea? Ariel hadn't heard from her since this mystery unfolded.

The Bookstore Proprietor

Nestled between the hardware store and the dry cleaners in a small storefront near the edge of town was Porter's Bookstore. A sign swung from the awning out front that read:

PORTER'S BOOKSTORE
SPECIALIZING IN RARE AND HARD TO FIND BOOKS
BUY – SELL – TRADE

Ariel and Lenny rolled up to the store and leaned their bikes against a pole. A bell chimed as they entered the shop. They were met with the same musty smell of old books that greeted them upon entering the library and the university.

The two looked around, taking in the vast collection of books for sell. The store was divided into sections marked by little signs that stood on top of some of the shelves. There was a section for classical literature, one for mysteries, another for science, and so forth. In the back, Ariel spotted a locked display stand under a RARE AND COLLECTIBLES sign.

"That must be where they keep their really expensive books," she said.

At the very front of the store, a crude counter held stacks of paperback books, papers, and folders. Behind the counter sat a dingy, out-dated cash register. Huge stacks of handwritten receipts and invoices filled the void next to the register.

"High tech this guy ain't," Lenny whispered.

Behind the counter a beaded curtain hung over an opening that led to the back room. Through this curtain a tall man with curly black hair and thick glasses emerged. He carried several paperbacks tucked under his arm.

Something seemed oddly familiar about him, but Ariel couldn't quite place it.

The man dropped his heavy load onto the counter. "May I help you?"

Ariel and Lenny stepped closer. "Are you Mr. Nate Porter?" Ariel asked.

"The one and only. What can I do you for? Looking for a book? You name it, I've got it—with the exception of old comic books, of course, which I keep to myself." Mr. Porter chuckled at his own joke. He seemed nice enough, although his humor could use a little work.

"Umm, my name is Ariel Hartman, and this is my brother Lenny. Actually, we're here looking more for information than a book."

Mr. Porter cocked his head to the side. "Oh? What kind of information?"

Ariel jumped right to the point. "Did you happen to hear about the theft at the museum the other night? It was a diary of a soldier signed by George Washington."

"I did hear about it," Mr. Porter said, sorting the paperbacks by author name. "What would you like to know?"

Lenny made his way to the graphic novels to leave the detective work to his sleuthing sister. Ariel rested her elbows on the counter. "Well, seeing as I hear you helped Mrs. Carmichael authencate—"

"Its *authenticate*," Mr. Porter said, smiling. "I helped her authenticate the diary."

"Authenticate," Ariel repeated. "Sorry about that. Anyway, you might know then why anyone would want to steal it."

Mr. Porter stopped sorting and looked up Ariel. His stare seemed to linger. "There are probably many reasons why someone would take it, but why are you so concerned about it?"

Ariel attempted to act casual as she thumbed through a mystery novel lying next to her. "We have a friend who may have seen the thief run away with the diary. Being as you are the expert on rare books, we thought you might help us better understand what's so great about this diary."

Mr. Porter tilted his head toward the ceiling. "Hmm. Let me see. I can tell you that Mrs. Carmichael called me a few weeks ago and told me that she had received a rare diary. She asked if I might check it out before she showcased it in the museum. She said that the diary was written by a soldier who came from this city. He gave an eyewitness account to events that occurred in the American Revolution, most notably, the Battle of Trenton. One distinguishing trait it possessed was George Washington's signature."

Ariel sighed. She already knew all this. She pressed for more information. "Yes, that's what Mrs. Carmichael said, but how do you go about examining a book's authenticity?"

Mr. Porter grabbed a handful of books from the stack he created and walked to a nearby bookshelf. "My job was to determine if the origin of the diary most likely matched its claim. I examined the book's binding, performed tests on the paper and ink, and verified the type of writing used, known as the script. Each item was commonly used in the 1700s. I also compared George Washington's signature to known signatures of Washington. It also seemed to check out."

"How much do you think a book like that might go for?"

Mr. Porter chuckled slightly. "You are full of questions aren't you? Grab me another stack of books over there, and I'll answer all of your questions."

Ariel reached for the remaining books and walked them over to him. She scanned the titles on the spines of the books. One title caught her attention: *To Catch a Thief* by David Dodge. Mr. Porter noticed Ariel's interest. He pulled it out and handed it to her. As she flipped through the pages, he said, "Talk about a rare find, that's one for ya. Just like the diary. It's hard to say how much the diary's worth though, but if I had to guess, I'd say upwards of $15,000."

Ariel stopped thumbing through the novel and gave it back to Mr. Porter. "My goodness. That is a lot of money. But I don't think it will break the bank." She looked around for Lenny and found him gazing into the rare and collectible book case. She heard him utter a "Wow" as he studied the case's contents.

"True, but there were some things that were even more unusual about this diary," Mr. Porter said, returning to the register area.

Ariel strolled toward him. "Really, like what?"

Pulling out a stool, Mr. Porter said, "There's this thing called provenance, which is a fancy word that describes an artifact's history and its ownership. The only record provided for the stolen diary was the letter that came from the attorney. It said the diary had been in the family for generations."

"That only adds to the mystery because the attorney guy seems to have just packed up and left," she said.

"He did? I didn't know about that. Anyway, there's more. You remember I said it was in excellent condition. Well, it was in *really* excellent condition, like someone preserved the book for a very long time—maybe even from the point it was written."

Lenny suddenly appeared next to Ariel. He lightly jabbed her in the arm with his elbow. "I said the same thing to the museum lady. It looked like new."

Mr. Porter nodded. "That's not the case in most situations. Most of the time it's only after several years that people begin to consider that something like this might one day be valuable. This diary was written during a war where certain measures to protect it was almost unheard of. Most would write journals during this time, but keeping it from getting soiled or exposed to the elements was difficult, if not impossible. It's like this thing was meant to be a keepsake. This, of course, only increases its value, but also makes such experts as myself very wary at face value that it is … well … real."

"Do you have any doubts that it's real, Mr. Porter?" Ariel half expected the diary to be a fake.

"Oh, no. I believe it is the real deal, yet it's still strange." Mr. Porter scratched his head.

The mystery about this diary deepened and Ariel felt no closer to understanding why anybody would want it so badly. "Is there anything else about the diary that seemed strange?"

"Yes, the dedication in the front." Mr. Porter squinted, straining to remember the words. "It reads: To Barney, may you find the treasure within that makest thy heart rich. Your dear comrade, Louis."

"What makes that so unusual?" she asked.

"Who do you know who dedicates their personal diaries to someone else? Aren't diaries full of personal notes and memories? It was as if this diary was intended to be shared."

"Maybe it was to a loved one or someone near to him."

"Maybe. Again, it was as if this diary was written for the sole purpose of protecting something. Like some valuable information or whatever, not just personal observations about the war or random thoughts like you'd expect to see in a diary. Also, the dedication is a little obscure. I read the contents, and I would not consider there to be a 'treasure' within."

Ariel tried her best to conceal her excitement. She felt even more certain that there was more to this diary than met the eye, and Mr. Porter had all but confirmed it. Was it possible that it held secrets that the thief was aware of? She had to know more about what was inside that diary and the person who wrote it. "One last question," she said. "Who is Louis?"

"According to the letter of authentication, his name is Louis Preston. All I can tell you for now is that he authored the diary."

"Well, thank you for your time," Ariel said. Lenny added his thanks.

"My pleasure," Mr. Porter said.

As the duo moved toward the exit, Lenny's elbow snagged the corner of one of the manila folders that rested on the top of the counter, knocking it to the floor. Paper flew in all directions.

"I am so sorry." Lenny blushed. He fell to his knees and started to scoop up the fallen papers.

Mr. Porter joined him on the floor and hurriedly began to shove the documents back into the folder.

While Lenny and Mr. Porter gathered paper, a page caught Ariel's eye. It appeared to be a copy of one of the pages from the diary—the one with the map. Her mind went into overdrive until she heard the chime of the door bell.

"You coming, or what?" Lenny said, propping the door open with his foot.

"Yeah, sorry," she said. Ariel turned back to say goodbye to Mr. Porter, but he was gone.

Outside, Ariel tugged on Lenny's arm with a firm grip. "I think Mr. Porter knows more than he's letting on." She glanced toward the window and spotted Mr. Porter watching them from behind the beaded curtain.

The Graveyard

A full moon cast a warm glow over the small town of Summerville. A light breeze picked up, chilling the night air. Ariel slipped her hands into the sleeves of her wind breaker and poked her head around the corner wall outside Porter's Bookstore.

Lenny pulled his hoodie over his head then leaned back against the wall. "So, why are we here again snooping on the book guy?"

Ariel pressed her finger against her mouth for Lenny to keep his voice down. "I told you already. This guy is hiding something and we are going to find out what it is."

Shoving his hands into his pants pocket for warmth, Lenny said, more quietly, "And all this is because he gave you a funny look earlier today?"

"Not just that, but why did he have a copy of that map?"

"I don't know. Maybe because he authcated the diary."

"*Authenticated*," Ariel corrected.

Lenny rolled his eyes. "Authcated. Authenticated. Whatever. And how did you get Mom to let us come out here after dark anyway?"

Ariel pulled a cell phone out of her jacket and held it up to Lenny. "I had to do some sweet talking, that's for sure. Finally, Mom gave me her phone and made me promise to call her every thirty minutes giving her every detail of where we are and what we are doing, or else."

"What are you going to tell her? 'Well, Mom, we're casing a joint right now and freezing our tails off, but I got a gut feeling about this because—'"

"Shh!" Ariel waved to Lenny to be quiet. "He's coming out now."

Mr. Porter eased out of the store and pulled the door shut. A dim glow from the awning lights illuminated his beige trench coat and brown Fedora hat. Mr. Porter locked the door and walked to his car where he popped open the trunk. He reached inside and pulled out a long stick with a triangle-shaped end.

"What is that?" Lenny said.

Mr. Porter moved back toward the light, and Ariel caught a glimpse of the item he carried. "It's a shovel," she said.

The book dealer flung the shovel over his shoulder and glanced in the direction of Ariel and Lenny's hiding spot. Mr. Porter's appearance jogged an important memory in Ariel's mind. "Lenny, from this angle, does Mr. Porter remind you of anybody?"

Lenny curled his lips. "I don't know. Looks like some creep with a shovel to me."

"Remember Chelsea's description of the thief? Beige coat, thick glasses, and a hat pulled low."

"Oh, yeah. Now that you mention it, he does fit the bill on that description. Do you think he's the guy?"

"It sure looks that way. Look," she said, pointing to Mr. Porter as he headed down the sidewalk away from the store. "He's going somewhere. Let's follow him."

Ariel waited until Mr. Porter was just far enough away where she didn't lose him in the darkness. Then she sprang from behind the wall and raced toward Mr. Porter's car where she dropped into a crouched position, her head bobbing just above the hood.

Lenny followed and slipped next to Ariel. "Where's he going?"

Ariel shook her head. "I don't know but we've got to find cover if we want to follow him." Ariel pointed to a tree just a few yards away. "Let's run to that tree over there."

Racing low to the ground, Ariel and Lenny ducked behind the tree's thick trunk. They dropped to their knees and watched Mr. Porter head into a grove of pine trees.

"He's going into the woods," Ariel said. She turned to her brother. "Where does that lead?"

Lenny rubbed his chin. "That either goes to the Miner's Creek or to the graveyard."

Lenny did not only have a grasp of mathematics, he had a keen since of direction. Ariel sometimes called him a walking GPS because he could find his way around so easily.

The duo trailed quietly behind Mr. Porter as he took the trail that led to the Summerville Cemetery. Ariel groaned. "I guess that answers our question. He's going to the graveyard."

Ariel started to follow but Lenny pulled her back.

"Wait" he said, in a hushed tone. "It looks like he's going around the back way. Let's circle around to the front and spread out. We can come up on his opposite side and cover more ground."

"Good idea," she said.

The two crept through the woodland area until they came to a gravel road that led to the cemetery entrance. The blackened outline of the wrought-iron gate loomed just ahead and seemed to emit an unwelcoming aura. Ariel and Lenny approached cautiously, the rocky road crunching under their shoes.

Ariel shivered more from dread than from the cold air that engulfed her. "This place gives me the creeps."

Lenny glanced back at her. "Why? Are you afraid of ghosts?"

"No!" she replied. "I don't believe in ghosts, unless it's the Holy Ghost. You know that. It's just that … well, I don't know what it is. It just creeps me out."

Lenny pulled on the gate, but it did not budge. He looked down and saw the padlock connected to a rusty chain that wrapped around the gate and the post. Lenny shook the lock in protest. "It's locked. Now what do we do?"

Ariel eased between the bars of the gate. She was thin enough to fit. But Lenny would not. She slid back out and surveyed the fence that ran along the front of the graveyard. Three strands of twisted barbed wire spaced several inches apart crowned the top. No way would Lenny be able to scale over those razor-sharp teeth. She walked the distance of the fence until she came to the corner. There she saw a shorter, somewhat dilapidated, chained fence that ran down the side of the cemetery. No barbed wires.

Ariel motioned for Lenny. "Look," she said. "You climb over and I'll go back through the front gate. I'll meet you inside."

She jogged back to the front, slid between the bars and raced back to her brother. She arrived just as Lenny fell over the top, landing on the ground with a sickening thud. "Are you all right?" Ariel asked.

Lenny grimaced and grabbed his back. "Couldn't be better," he moaned. He gingerly rose to his feet and brushed the dirt and leaves from his jeans. "Where to now?"

Ariel turned and saw a forest of headstones that stood all around like miniature odd-shaped trees. Suddenly, in the distance she spotted a faint beam of light that danced from side to side and moved slowly toward the back of the graveyard.

"Over there!" she said, pointing.

"I see it," said Lenny. "It seems Mr. Porter was the smart one to think to bring a flashlight." He waved to his right. "I will go this direction, and come around this side." He pointed to his left. "You go around that way. And be careful. Don't get too close, Ariel. Okay?"

"I won't," she said.

Lenny got right in Ariel's face, almost touching nose-to-nose. "Promise?" he said.

Ariel pushed him away. "I promise, all right?"

Lenny nodded and then dashed off.

Standing alone in a graveyard at night brought Ariel a strong sense of anxiety. She felt that her heart rose from her chest and now lodged in her ears, pounding loudly with quickened beats. Without thinking, almost automatically, she started praying. "Oh, Jesus. Please. Please. Please. Keep us safe."

Her heart slowed and she felt her courage return. She turned to see if Lenny was still in sight, but she was absolutely and completely alone—with the exception of the peace she felt after her short prayer. Ariel took a deep breath and set off toward the beam of light.

The Buried Trunk

Ariel dropped to the ground. She hid behind a tombstone topped by a chubby cement angel. She poked her head around the cold concrete structure and spied Mr. Porter's movements.

He came to a section of the graveyard enclosed by a pointy iron fence. The hinges of the swinging gate squeaked as he pushed it open. He waved the flashlight until its beam fell on one particular grave marker. Slowly, he approached the grave and then stooped down, tracing a finger along the headstone's inscription. In one fluid motion, Mr. Porter rose to his feet and made an about-face. Then, almost robot-like, he walked back the way he came taking long, measured steps.

Ariel's eyes followed him until he came to an abrupt halt near an old ramshackle chapel. With Mr. Porter's back to her, she dashed toward the grave marker where he began his curious stroll.

Going through the gate was out of the question given the noise it made when Mr. Porter walked through it. So, she went the back way. Ariel carefully straddled the fence and squeezed around its sharp-pointed pillars.   Then she crept over to the grave and knelt beside the headstone. She tried to make out the inscription, but with little light and after centuries of weather, it was impossible to read the words. Like Mr. Porter, she ran her fingers inside the etching and thought she felt an E – L – I – Z form against her fingertips.

Realizing she was in plain view if Mr. Porter should decide to return, Ariel slipped behind the headstone.

Mr. Porter was just a dark outline against the faint moonlight where he stood near the old chapel. But Ariel watched as he lifted the shovel and plunged it deep into the ground. Minutes later, he lowered both hands into the hole he had just dug where he pulled out a small dome-topped box that resembled an old-timey luggage trunk.

"What is that?" Ariel said to herself. *Could it be a baby's coffin?* She had to get a closer look. Ariel quickly vaulted the pointed fence. Quietly she sprinted from tombstone to tombstone until she was within fifty feet of Mr. Porter.

He reached into his coat pocket and withdrew a long skeleton key. Holding the flashlight between his teeth, he aimed the beam toward a rusted padlock on the front of the box and thrust the key into the lock. After several forced twists, the lock finally unlatched. Mr. Porter quickly pulled the padlock from the box and tossed it to the side. He then pried the lid open, reached into the belly of the box, and removed a chunk of rock. When he shined his light on it, the stone began to glisten and sparkle.

After placing the object back into the box, he slammed the lid shut and shoved the lock into his coat pocket. Mr. Porter heaved the box onto his shoulder and picked up the shovel.

As he turned to leave, the cell phone in Ariel's coat rang. Her heart sank. She had forgotten to call her mom. No doubt Mom was calling her. She grabbed the phone and quickly punched the "ignore" button. Ariel held her breath and hoped Mr. Porter did not hear.

But he did. He swung his flashlight in Ariel's direction. "Who's there?" he shouted.

Ariel squeezed her eyes shut and waited. A wave of dread washed over her and flooded her stomach. She knew that at any minute she would be discovered.

Caught

Ariel pulled her knees to her chin and pressed firmly against the back of the tombstone. She slowed her breathing so she could listen for Mr. Porter's approaching foot falls.

She heard the soft snapping of a twig. Ariel could not tell where the sound came from but it had to be close. Suddenly, she was blinded by light. She shielded her eyes and tried to make out the features of the man clutching the flashlight.

"Stay there, Ariel," the man said.

The voice was not Mr. Porter's, but—

"Detective Sloan?" Ariel asked, surprised.

The detective stepped closer and motioned for her to remain still. He then drew his gun and extended it toward Mr. Porter. "Freeze!"

Ariel poked her head up. She watched Mr. Porter drop the shovel to the ground and surrender, his arms raised high above his head.

Detective Sloan grabbed his radio and called for backup.

Minutes later, Detective Sloan helped the cuffed Mr. Porter into the back seat of Officer Frazier's squad car. "He's all yours," he said, slamming the door. Detective Sloan then leaned into the car through the open passenger-side window. "Take him to the police station and get him booked. I'll be there soon to question him after I've had a chance to talk to these kids."

Officer Frazier nodded and then eased the car onto the gravel road.

Detective Sloan turned and walked to his car where Ariel and Lenny quietly sat in the back, the doors open on either side like wings on a bird.

Ariel wished she was a bird at that moment so she could soar far from this place. First, she got an ear full from her Mom for not calling her back as promised, compounded by having to fess up to what she and Lenny had been doing. Now, she could tell by the look on Detective Sloan's face she had another ear full coming.

Detective Sloan tossed his hat onto the trunk of his car and ran his fingers through his hair. He bent down next to Ariel and sighed. "I'm not the smartest cookie in the world, but you being out here sure looks to me more like you chasing the thief than doing Internet research like we agreed to. What do you think?"

"I guess I got a little carried away," Ariel said.

"I'd have to agree with you there. Still, you seem to have a knack for figuring things out. What led you to suspect Nate Porter anyway?"

Ariel shifted in her seat. "When we went to visit him earlier today to get information about what the value of the diary might be worth, I saw he had a copy of the map from the diary. I told Lenny he was hiding something but I didn't know what. I guess I was right."

Detective Sloan shook his head. "You know, you really take the cake. If it hadn't been for an anonymous tip that someone was lurking around the graveyard, you and your brother might have become its next permanent residents."

Lenny turned and glared at Ariel.

Ariel felt Lenny's eyes burn into her. She let her shoulders droop and drew in a deep breath. "Maybe this isn't a good time to ask, but what's in the box?"

"Don't know yet." Detective Sloan stood and slipped his hat back onto his head. "I tell you what, since you got us this far in the case, come by the police station tomorrow and I'll let you know." He pulled out a sheet of paper from his shirt pocket. "In the meantime, see if you make anything out from this." He handed the paper to Ariel. She glanced down at what was scrawled across the crumbled sheet:

Galatians 6:2 Bear ye one another's burdens, and so fulfil the law of Christ.

Galatians 1:18 Then after three years I went up to Jerusalem to see Peter, and abode with him fifteen days.

Galatians 1:2 And all the brethren which are with me, unto the churches of Galatia:

Galatians 5:11 And I, brethren, if I yet preach circumcision, why do I yet suffer persecution? then is the offence of the cross ceased.

Galatians 5:16 This I say then, Walk in the Spirit, and ye shall not fulfil the lust of the flesh.

Galatians 1:18 Then after three years I went up to Jerusalem to see Peter, and abode with him fifteen days.

Galatians 1:1 Paul, an apostle, (not of men, neither by man, but by Jesus Christ, and God the Father, who raised him from the dead;

Galatians 3:28 There is neither Jew nor Greek, there is neither bond nor free, there is neither male nor female: for ye are all one in Christ Jesus.

Galatians 1:13 For ye have heard of my conversation in time past in the Jews' religion, how that beyond measure I persecuted the church of God, and wasted it:

Galatians 1:13 For ye have heard of my conversation in time past in the Jews' religion, how that beyond measure I persecuted the church of God, and wasted it:

Galatians 5:1 Stand fast therefore in the liberty wherewith Christ hath made us free, and be not entangled again with the yoke of bondage.

Galatians 1:13 For ye have heard of my conversation in time past in the Jews' religion, how that beyond measure I persecuted the church of God, and wasted it:

Galatians 1:18 Then after three years I went up to Jerusalem to see Peter, and abode with him fifteen days.

Galatians 4:2 But is under tutors and governors until the time appointed of the father.

She looked up at Detective Sloan, bewildered. "It's just a bunch of verses from Galatians."

"That's right," he said. "Mr. Porter had it on him when I arrested him. You're a good church-going girl. Maybe you can help me figure it out."

Ariel tried to hold back her smile under the circumstances, but she couldn't control herself. She grinned like a kid opening presents on Christmas morning.

Shiny Green Things

The next morning, Ariel sat alone in INTERROGATION ROOM 2 waiting for Detective Sloan. Only a single table and three mismatched plastic chairs occupied the small space. She kept folding and unfolding the sheet of paper the detective gave her at the cemetery. At first glance, it was just a random list of verses from Galatians. But over breakfast, Ariel spotted the pattern.

While she waited, she thought about Lenny. He was too upset last night to talk to her. On the bike ride home, he trailed far behind Ariel. At home, he went straight to his room when they arrived with no good-night. She considered waking him this morning, but when she slipped into his room, she found him sprawled across the bed sound asleep, a video-game controller in his hand and the monitor flashing a race car paused in the middle of the track. She left him to sleep.

She even tried calling Chelsea, the third time this week. Again, no answer. Ariel decided two messages were enough, so she hung up when she heard the recorder begin to play. Was Chelsea dodging her calls? Was something else wrong?

Ariel stirred when the door opened. Detective Sloan came in bearing a mud-encrusted old trunk. He set it on the table and gently pried the lid back.

"Is that what Mr. Porter dug up?" she said.

"Uh-huh," he replied, removing its contents. Inside were a set of letters tied in a bundle by a red silk ribbon, a large Bible, a journal, and a pouch made of some kind of animal skin drawn tight by a leather string. He loosened the draw string and turned the pouch upside down over his hand. A rock with shiny green crystals fell into his palm.

Ariel sprang from her chair. She stared down at the dazzling piece of stone. "Are those what I think they are?"

"Yep," he said, curling his lips. "This is an emerald ore, and those are real emeralds."

"They are beautiful, but they sure are small. Is it worth a lot of money?"

"These are worth a couple of thousand, but it seems like a lot of trouble to go through for this and a few books and letters, don't you think?" He slid the emerald-encrusted stone back into the pouch and tossed it onto the table.

"Maybe there's more where that came from." She pointed to the other items pulled from the box. "Have you gone through this other stuff yet?"

Detective Sloan eased into a chair and reached for the journal. "We tried to, but it's written in that old English-style script and badly faded." He carefully turned a page in the leather-bound book. "We are trying to find someone who can decipher this stuff."

"I bet Dr. Smith can help," Ariel suggested.

Detective Sloan looked up from the book. "Dr. Smith? Is he a professor at your dad's college?"

Ariel nodded. "He teaches history mostly, but he helped Lenny and me to understand a little more about the diary's value. At least what he could because he said he didn't know much specifics about the diary itself. But he may be able to read this for you."

"Alright, I'll give him a call." Detective Sloan began to return the items to the box. "Any luck with those verses from Galatians?"

Ariel pushed the sheet toward Detective Sloan. "It took some doing, but I think I figured it out."

"Great. Enlighten me," Detective Sloan said, grasping the paper.

"At first I thought maybe there was some pattern in what the verses said, but I decided against that when I saw that Mr. Porter had written Galatians 1:13 and Galatians 1:18 three times each."

"Could be there's a pattern to the verse references," Detective Sloan offered.

"Thought about that too, but it dawned on me over my bowl of oatmeal."

Detective Sloan laughed. "I always thought oatmeal was good for the brain. But I had no idea."

Ariel rolled her eyes playfully. "Seriously, when I had a chance to look it over at breakfast, I saw something interesting." Ariel tapped the list. "If you look hard, you'll see that Mr. Porter drew a faint pencil line through some of the words."

"I see it," Detective Sloan said.

"Put the words together and you get BEAR-FIFTEEN-WITH-CROSS-WALK-THREE-AND-ONE-PAST-CHURCH-STAND-MEA-SURE-THREE-UNDER."

"That makes no sense. What does it mean?"

"When you form them into sentences, it's 'Bear fifteen with cross. Walk three and one past church. Stand, measure three under.' See the words 'bear', 'walk' and 'stand' are capitalized in the verses? I'm sure that means the start of a different phrase or sentence."

"Okay, but still, what does it mean?"

Ariel fell back into her chair. "It sounds like directions to a treasure, or something. There's a chapel in the cemetery. That could be a church. And there are crosses all over the cemetery. This is probably what Mr. Porter used to help him find the trunk."

Detective Sloan frowned, staring at the weathered box in front of him. "Some treasure."

"Yeah, looks that way ... unless ...." Ariel got that far-away look.

"Unless what?"

"Unless this is just one of another clue that leads to a bigger treasure." Ariel brushed off the comment. "Anyway, I'm sure Mr. Porter can tell you more."

"Hmph. He's not talking. He said he did nothing wrong and won't offer much information."

"Didn't do anything wrong?" Ariel said, mockingly. "When's stealing a diary not wrong?"

"Well, that's just the thing. We can't find the diary. We've searched his shop, his apartment, his car ... everywhere, and we can't find it."

Ariel rose and began pacing. "What if he sold the diary? Dr. Smith about accused him of having criminal connections through his bookstore to sell the diary illegally."

Detective Sloan smiled. "I like the way you think. We're checking that angle now. But all we've got him on is trespassing and destruction of private property. No proof he took the diary. We're only going to be able to hold him for another twenty-four hours, and then it's likely he'll make bail."

"What about the attorney that vanished after sending the diary? Any new leads on him?"

Shaking his head, Detective Sloan said, "Nope. We are still running that down. I had hoped to hear from Chelsea's mom about that. She promised to look into those attorney databases she has access to, but no answer yet."

"Yeah, I've been trying to reach Chelsea with no luck." Ariel said.

"My hunch is this attorney never existed or he's an accomplice in all of this that's still out there somewhere. Of course, Mr. Porter's not saying a word."

Ariel grinned at Detective Sloan. "I've got an idea!"

Detective Sloan moaned. "This isn't going to involve me having to rescue you again, will it?"

"No," Ariel said laughingly. "I'm going to check something out with Mrs. Carmichael. But I've got a question. Mr. Porter seemed awfully interested in one particular grave in that old section of the cemetery. I ran my fingers along the name and it felt like E-L-I-Z. Doesn't ring a bell, does it?"

Detective Sloan laced his fingers behind his head and closed his eyes. "There's an Elizabeth Walker who's buried there. She was one of the founders of Summerville."

"That's it!" Ariel said, snapping her fingers. "I think a little history lesson with Mrs. Carmichael will shed some light on this mystery."

Detective Sloan gave a slight chuckle. "Why are you so interested in looking for more clues? We've got our guy. He's sitting in a cell right down the hall. It's just a matter of time till we find the diary and link this all back to him."

"It's all about finding the truth," she said. "That's one of the reasons I love being a Christian. I just love truth, and I love digging to find the truth."

"I believe that about you. I can tell you've got a God-given gift. But I love finding the truth too." Detective Sloan stood, grabbed the trunk, and walked toward the door. He reached for the door knob and said, "And you want to know how I find the truth?"

"How?" Ariel asked.

"I uncover the lies. You get rid of all the lies and all that's left is the truth." He smiled as he opened the door and motioned Ariel out of the room.

Back to the Beginning

The police station occupied the same building as the Courthouse and City Hall, a gleaming white structure with stately Corinthian columns overlooking a beautifully manicured lawn in the center of the town square. Ariel bounced down the front steps, breathing in the fragrant air of flowers blossoming in the garden. It was the dawn of another spring season. This time of year seemed to invigorate her mind, especially after a long, cold winter.

This was a good thing because this case kept getting more complex. True, the police may very well have the thief locked up. But what link did the diary have to that trunk of old memories and the precious rock dug up by Mr. Porter? And, for that matter, where was the diary?

Ariel could not rest until all the clues fit neatly together like a completed puzzle. There were too many pieces still missing for her to be satisfied. The one thing that seemed to surface time and again pointed to some connection with Summerville's beginnings. Both the author of the diary and the person whose grave most captured Mr. Porter's attention were founders of the town. The one person who knew about Summerville's history was Mrs. Carmichael.

Moments later, Ariel breezed past Madge at the museum registration desk on her way to Mrs. Carmichael's office. She stood nervously at the curator's door. Mental images of her getting caught snooping around the display case the last time she was there flashed through Ariel's brain. She forced back the memories, whispered a prayer, and knocked.

Behind the door, Ariel heard the faint squeak of a chair being rolled back followed by the clatter of approaching footsteps. The door swung open, and there stood Mrs. Carmichael, glasses tottering on the tip of her nose.

"Oh, my," Mrs. Carmichael said, surprised. She then peered down at Ariel. "It's you again. What can I do for you?"

Ariel's face flushed and she felt her mouth suddenly grow dry. She cleared her throat. "I am so sorry to bother you, Mrs. Carmichael, but it's quite important. By now I'm sure you've heard that Mr. Porter has been arrested and is believed to have stolen the diary."

Mrs. Carmichael blinked. "I had not heard that." She extended her arm toward an empty chair in front of her desk. "Care to come in?"

Ariel smiled as she stepped inside the office. Many of the piles of paper were cleared away and she could actually see the top of Mrs. Carmichael's desk.

The curator noticed the look of astonishment on Ariel's face. "I've been doing some cleaning lately. I've found it very therapeutic. It's helped take my mind off the matter of the theft." She motioned again at the chair. "Please sit and tell me all about what you've learned."

Ariel told Mrs. Carmichael about discovering a copy of the diary's map at Porter's Bookstore and the chest of old books, papers, and emerald stones found by Mr. Porter. She also explained how the list of verses on Mr. Porter when he was arrested was actually a secret code that led him to the old trunk.

Mrs. Carmichael listened intently, stopping Ariel a couple of times to ask questions. After Ariel finished, Mrs. Carmichael said, "That is some story. I'm shocked that it was Mr. Porter. To think I trusted him."

"That's just the thing," Ariel said. "The police have searched his apartment and his bookstore, and they have not found the diary. He may have already sold it, but there's a chance he didn't take it. That's why I'm here. I'm thinking this all ties somehow to the early founders of Summerville. I know you could provide details about that."

"Yes, of course. What would you like to know?"

"For starters, what's the connection between Louis Preston and Elizabeth Walker?" Ariel asked.

"They were brother and sister."

"That is interesting. A family connection. I had not thought about that. How did they come to Summerville?"

"Their parents were wealthy colonial land owners. As most influential people before the war, they were loyal to the throne of England. That allegiance soon cost them everything. The revolutionists seized their land, and soon after they died in a bizarre accident. I don't know the details, only that they were ambushed while traveling on horseback into town. With their family in chaos and left penniless, Louis and Elizabeth set out to find a new place to live, as far from the political unrest as possible."

"I don't understand then why Louis would later want to fight in the war, especially on the same side of those that did this to their parents."

"Its funny you should ask that question because I've often wondered the same thing. Let me show you something." Mrs. Carmichael went to one of her filing cabinets. She opened the top drawer and pulled out a folder. "Take a look at this," she said, handing a sheet of paper to Ariel.

Ariel glanced over the document. "It looks like a marriage certificate."

Mrs. Carmichael gave a slight nod. "That's right. It's Elizabeth's. But look at the name of the man she married."

Ariel ran her finger along the page searching for the name. "I think it says Barnabus Walker."

"You are correct. And, do you know what is short for Barnabus?" Mrs. Carmichael asked.

Ariel gasped. "Barney! But didn't Louis dedicate the diary to a Barney?"

A grin spread across the curator's face. "That's right. And I've been doing a little research on Mr. Barnabus Walker since you asked about him when I showed you those photographs of the diary. Not only did I discover he was Elizabeth's husband, but it turns out he was a fiery speaker against what he called the oppressive British regime. He convinced many young men to take up arms and fight for independence. He even convinced one Louis Preston."

"So, Elizabeth fell in love with someone who could have been her enemy, considering what was done to her parents."

Mrs. Carmichael giggled. "Oh dear child, what love will do. It covers a multitude of sins."

That may be true, thought Ariel, staring into space and twirling her hair. But something else seemed to be covering up a lot of answers to a lot of questions, and it all came back to that diary. She turned to Mrs. Carmichael and said, "Do you think I can borrow those photographs? I promise to return them safe and sound."

"Well, since you promised to be careful, you can," Mrs. Carmichael said.

"Oh, I promise," Ariel said.

While Mrs. Carmichael reached into her desk drawer, Ariel caught sight of a photograph on the wall, hidden the last time she and Lenny were there by a tall stack of books. Ariel pointed to the picture, "What is that, Mrs. Carmichael?"

The curator swiveled in her chair. "That is our Board of Trustees. You might recognize a few people. There's me, of course, then there's the former mayor, Dr. Smith from the university, and a few business people and former city council members that you might not recognize." She spun around and handed Ariel a thick folder. "Here are the photographs. Again, please be careful. These are my only copies."

Ariel thanked Mrs. Carmichael and left. She glanced at the clock above the museum exit and was surprised that it was ten minutes until noon. She was already on Mom's bad side. No need to make matters worse by not showing up for lunch.

The Ignored Warning

When Ariel arrived at home, she found a note on the kitchen table:

There are cold cuts in the bottom drawer of the refrigerator. Need to make yourself a sandwich. I've got a Ladies Auxiliary meeting at the church until 2.

Love,
Mom

Great. Ariel didn't have to rush home after all. Since she was already there, she decided to make a sandwich anyway and think about her next move.

Ariel grabbed the package of ham and the bottle of mustard from the refrigerator. She had begun spreading some mustard on a piece of bread when the phone rang. Ariel jumped, dropping the knife onto the floor with a clatter. She raced to the phone to check the Caller ID. CALLER BLOCKED. Probably a sales call. She let it go to voicemail.

The answering machine beeped, and the recording started. Ariel listened for the message through the microphone. There was a long period of silence followed by a husky voice that came onto the line. "Drop it, little Sherlock, if you know what's good for you!" Then *click* followed by the dead sound of dial tone.

Ariel stood frozen, stunned by the stern warning. She looked back at the half-prepared sandwich and suddenly lost her appetite. She put the food back into the refrigerator, tossed the knife into the sink, and pushed PLAY on the answering machine. Ariel listened to the recording several times, trying to pin-point subtle inflections in the voice in hopes of recognizing the caller's identity. No luck.

The threat only roused her curiosity. She snatched the stack of photographs from the folder and hurriedly flipped through them. There was only one she really wanted: the map. When she found it, she shoved the photograph into her back pocket and went to the kitchen junk drawer in search of a pen and a scratch piece of paper.

While she rummaged through the drawer, Lenny walked into the kitchen behind her. He ran his hand through his mangled hair and yawned. "What are you doing?" he asked sleepily.

Ariel spun around so fast she pulled out the drawer. Paperclips, coupons, refrigerator magnets, and all sorts of stuff that no one really knew what to do with spilled onto the floor.

"You seem a little jumpy this morning," Lenny said.

"Lenny! You scared me. And it's not morning. It's afternoon." She bent down to pick up the mess.

Lenny reached for a bowl in the cabinet. "Morning. Afternoon. Whatever. It's Spring Break. Who cares?" he said, shaking a box of corn flakes over the empty bowl.

Ariel liked that he was talking to her, even if he was being sarcastic. She knew he had a right to be upset with her. She did promise to stay clear of Mr. Porter at the cemetery and didn't. But how was it her fault that her cell phone rang? Still, this was conversation, Lenny-style. She decided to test if all was forgiven.

Ariel bit the bottom of her lip, then said, "So, I'm about to do a little more investigating. You up?"

Lenny glared at Ariel with a you've-got-to-be-joking stare. His eyes darted toward the flashing light on the answering machine indicating there was a message. He walked over and pushed PLAY.

Ariel grimaced while she listened again to the sinister recording.

Lenny slowly turned toward Ariel and scoffed. "So, even after this, you still want to go investigating?" He plopped into a chair at the kitchen table, shaking his head in disbelief.

Ariel reached across the counter and quickly hit the ERASE key on the answering machine. "So I guess this means you're not coming."

Lenny hovered over his bowl of cereal ignoring Ariel.

"Fine. I'll go alone. God forbid my big brother would be there to protect me."

Lenny shrugged.

Ariel turned and charged from the room.

Ariel rolled up to the front of the cemetery. Sunlight filtered through the swaying trees and made the place a little less forbidden than at night. The gate stood open as if welcoming visitors with open arms. She leaned her bike against the fence and walked in.

After a quick survey of the lay of the graveyard, Ariel found the older section partitioned off by an iron fence where Summerville's early inhabitants were buried. Several yards away from there stood an ivy-ridden chapel that hundreds of years ago served as the community's only church. Ariel shielded her eyes and could just make out the faint outline of the hole dug by Mr. Porter. Suddenly, a man on a riding lawnmower towing a trailer of dirt drove from behind the church. The caretaker, no doubt, planning to fill the hole.

Ariel made her way toward Elizabeth Walker's grave. Standing next to her headstone, Ariel pulled from her pocket the picture of the hand-drawn map. She traced her fingers along a dotted line that ran between a single cross and a building with a small cross penciled on the roof. The similarity between the map and the graveyard was uncanny. Taken with the directions supplied by the list of verses from Galatians, it became obvious to Ariel that the diary was much more than just a first-hand account of war.

Next, Ariel knelt at the headstone. She withdrew a scrap of paper and pen from her front pocket and jotted down Elizabeth's name, birthday, and date of death.

She moved to the next grave on her right, not surprised to find that it was Barnabus Walker's, Elizabeth's husband. What she saw though etched in granite surprised her. His date of death was very close to Elizabeth's. To the left of Elizabeth's grave stood the headstone for Louis Preston, badly marred by years of neglect and weather. Ariel wrote down the information from his headstone on her scrap of paper.

Ariel glanced back at each of the tombstones checking her notes for accuracy against the inscriptions. As her eyes fell away from Barnabus's grave marker, another caught her attention. She crawled on her hands and knees toward the headstone that read MICAH WALKER. She studied his date of birth and re-checked her notes—only a few days apart from Elizabeth's death. Could this be Elizabeth and Barnabus' son, born so close to his own parents' demise?

She quickly wrote down Micah's information and moved down the line of gravestones, making note of the names and dates. Armed with these details, Ariel ran for her bike. Next stop: the library's genealogy records to flesh out a family tree.

Little did she know she was being watched.

Family Ties

The Summerville Library prided itself on offering the best genealogical department in the county with access to the National Archives and the Library of Congress, as well as an extensive collection of census records and files on land owner-ship, military service, marriages, and births going back to the *Mayflower*. Ariel used the Genealogy section for a research project at school where she had to trace her own family history. So, she had knowledge about how to quickly navigate her way through the data to identify Louis and Elizabeth's family trees, made even easier because she had a ready-made list of names with which to begin.

Ariel stood at the front desk and waited for the librarian to look up from her book long enough to offer help. When Ariel had her attention, she handed the library volunteer her card. In exchange, she was given an access card to all of the historical records. Ariel thanked the lady and hurried off to the Genealogy section.

Tucked behind a maze of tall shelves full of musty old books stood small cubicles with computers and microfiche machines. Ariel chose a computer near the back wall. She ran her access card through the card reader. As files began to appear on the monitor, she spread the notes she took at the cemetery on the desk beside her.

Ariel did not take long to trace Elizabeth Preston Walker's family. The results, though, sent chills down her spine. The screen displayed a series of names branching out like brackets in a sports tournament. One name near the end of the list caught her attention: Nathaniel Porter. Mr. Porter was in the bloodline of the sister to the diary's author. Ariel recalled that the letter from the attorney stated that the diary had been in the family for generations. But if it was Nate Porter's family that held the diary in safekeeping all this time, what motive did he have to steal it? Ariel hit PRINT and then set to work on the author.

Unraveling Louis Preston's family lineage proved more challenging for Ariel. She got as far as Orville and Henry Smythe, sons of Jacob and Ellen Smythe, and could go no further. Records of their ancestry had all but disappeared.

She began to play with her hair and think about how to get the information she needed to complete the trace. After a while, an image from her history textbook came to her mind. It was of a man draped in a leather apron swinging a huge hammer over an anvil with a caption that read YE OLDE BLACKSMYTHE.

With this new clue, Ariel typed a series of commands into the computer. She held her breath as the screen slowly began to build new branches on Louis' family tree. Excitement boiled inside as Ariel glanced over the names. She soon found another person she knew.

Her finger hovered over the PRINT key just as fingers not her own holding a foul-smelling cloth reached from behind and covered her nose. A second later, Ariel's world went black.

The Search for Ariel

"Where's Ariel?" Mrs. Hartman said, standing in the doorway to Lenny's bedroom. "She needs to get ready for mid-week service."

Lenny lay on his stomach across his bed. He stared intently at his monitor, attacking a video game controller with his thumbs. "I don't know where she's at. Probably on the scent of some criminal like an old bloodhound, I suppose."

"I don't like it," Mom said. "If she's not home by 7:00 PM, I'm calling your father."

At 7:45 PM with no sign of Ariel, her parents called the police station to report her missing.

Detective Sloan arrived at the Hartman's house minutes later. He tipped his hat to Dr. and Mrs. Hartman as he ambled through the front door. Dr. Hartman pointed him toward the living room and motioned for the detective to take the recliner while he sat next to his wife on the couch, throwing a comforting arm around her. Worried expressions painted their sullen faces.

Lenny eased down the stairs. He sat on the bottom step with full view of the adults and within earshot of their conversation.

"Dr. and Mrs. Hartman, I will tell you that we will do everything we can to find Ariel." Detective Sloan said. He flipped open a notepad. "Any information you have that might help us would be appreciated."

Mrs. Hartman dabbed her eye with a tissue. "Lenny told us about a threatening phone message left on the answering machine today," she said.

Detective Sloan's pencil froze on the notepad. He looked up and said, "Threatening message? May I hear it?"

Dr. Hartman shook his head. "Unfortunately, Ariel erased it. But it said something to the effect of, 'Stay away if you know what's good for you.'"

"Any idea who might have left it?"

"No," Dr. Hartman replied. "We were hoping you might know. We heard you arrested Mr. Porter. Any chance he might have anything to do with this?"

"I doubt it. He's still in jail waiting to make bail, and any calls from the police station would have come collect." Detective Sloan closed his notepad and stood. "I have every patrol officer out looking for Ariel. Chances are she's gotten into her detective persona and lost track of time."

"I don't think so," Mrs. Hartman said. "No matter how … active … she gets in one of her little cases, she hardly ever misses church. Tonight is mid-week service, and she'd be there if something wasn't wrong." She drew her hand to her mouth and forced back tears.

A static-filled voice came through the detective's walkie-talkie. "Detective Sloan, you there?"

Detective Sloan tilted his head toward the voice piece and pushed the button to talk. "Yeah, Bernice. I'm here with the Hartmans. What do you need?"

"We got a report from the library of an abandoned bike. You want me to send Officer Frazier over?"

"No. I'll check it out. Be there in five minutes."

Dr. Hartman jumped to his feet. "I'm coming with you," he said.

The detective held up his hands, palms out. "I've got this, Dr. Hartman. You stay here with your wife."

"I just can't stay here and do nothing," Ariel's father protested. "I must insist that I go."

Mrs. Hartman reached for her husband's hand and looked at the detective. "I will be okay. I do much better on my knees alone in prayer. I'll start calling people from our church to help me pray."

Detective Sloan reluctantly nodded.

Lenny did not stick around long enough to find out how the matter of his father going with Detective Sloan got settled. He had already slipped out of the house.

Locked Up!

The first thought that passed through Ariel's brain when she awoke was noticing the dull pain that spread through her head. Her second thought was the overwhelming sense of dread brought on by the darkness that engulfed her. She blinked several times, as much to relieve the pain as to focus her vision.

She lay on her back on a cold, dank floor. When her eyes finally adjusted to the dim light around her, she found herself staring up at rough-hewn beams that crisscrossed the ceiling.

Ariel tried to stand, but her legs felt wobbly. She reached for something solid nearby and grabbed the end of a long oak bench, one of many that surrounded her on either side of a narrow aisle. Along each wall, faint shards of light filtered through boarded-up stained-glass windows. Ariel looked toward the front of the room and saw a pulpit in the center of a wooden platform.

She realized she was in a small, primitive church. But where?

Stepping lightly as to not aggravate her aching head, she walked to one of the windows. Ariel leaned down and peeked through a small opening in one of the boards that was nailed to the sill. She stared at odd-shaped concrete crosses, statues, and tombstones.

"I'm in the cemetery chapel," she whispered to herself.

Ignoring the throbbing in her skull, she raced for the doors at the back of the building. She pulled and pulled at the handles, but the doors did not budge.

She dropped to the floor letting the tears pour from her swollen eyes. "Oh dear God, help me! Help me!" she prayed.

Breakthroughs and Setbacks

"Yes sir," replied the plain-looking library worker, a slight quiver in her voice. She was perturbed when she was interrupted in the part of her romance novel where Julio was just about to propose to Emily. The irritation turned to shock and embarrassment when she looked up sternly from her book to stare into a police officer's badge. Of course, she saw nothing and heard nothing, and it wasn't her who reported the bike. She told Detective Sloan that Mrs. Thompson, the head librarian, must have called on her way home for the evening. She at least remembered checking out an access card to a slender girl with the deepest blue eyes she ever saw, which reminded her of a character from one of her favorite books.

The librarian pulled up the records on her computer and found that a unit was still logged in under the access code she had provided Ariel earlier that day. She offered to escort the detective and Ariel's father to the workstation Ariel had been using.

"Did anybody else have access to these computers, or was anyone back here with Ariel?" Detective Sloan asked.

"No sir, I don't think so," she replied. "Of course, this section is open to the public; only the computers need an access card. She was the only one I issued a card to today."

"Is there anyway to bring up what she was looking at?"

The library worker typed a few keystrokes and then leaned toward the monitor. "Looks like it timed out and erased whatever she was working on. Wait a minute!" She pointed a finger in the air. "I think I saw on my computer out front that she made a print. We record the number of prints because the first ten pages are free. After that, it's ten cents per page. Maybe the pages she printed are still there."

"Where's the printer?" asked Dr. Hartman.

"It's right over here. Let me go check it out." Seconds later the librarian returned carrying three sheets of paper. She handed them to Detective Sloan.

The detective quickly scanned the sheets. "What am I looking at?"

"It's a family tree for an Elizabeth Walker." She scratched her head. "Where do I know that name?" she said more to herself than to anyone else.

"She's one of the founders of Summerville," Detective Sloan said.

Dr. Hartman held out his hand. "May I see that?" he asked. The detective gave him the papers, which Dr. Hartman carefully studied in a professorial manner. "Ah yes, it shows here that Elizabeth Walker was related to our very own Nathaniel Porter, our famous bookstore proprietor, no less."

"What's that?" Detective Sloan said, snatching the pages away from Ariel's father.

Dr. Hartman tapped on Mr. Porter's name. "Right here. Plain as day."

Detective Sloan ripped the intercom from his shoulder. "Bernice, this is Sloan. Tell Frazier or whoever's on duty to pull Porter out of his cell and get him over to Interrogation, pronto. I'm coming over there right now, and I'm going to get that character to talk."

"Hold on a sec, detective," Bernice said. There was a long silence before she came back on the line. "Sorry, Sloan, but he made bail. He was released over an hour ago."

Lenny wandered the darkened streets on his bicycle, trying to predict where his sister could have gone. He passed by the library and saw her bike parked in the rack. No need to check that. He knew she wasn't there, and Detective Sloan had that angle covered.

The last twenty-four hours played over and over in his mind like a bad movie. He wished he could take back his cold-shoulder treatment toward Ariel. What he regretted most of all was not going with Ariel when she left the house.

With the roles reversed and he now playing junior detective, he had to think like Ariel. What was she likely looking for at the library that could offer some clue to what might have happened to her? Did the sinister message left on the answering machine shed any light on this matter?

Lenny came up with zilch. Left with no other option, he decided to revisit all the places they investigated, starting with Porter's Bookstore.

The store was dark except for the overhead fluorescent bulbs hanging over the covered walkway out front. Lenny jumped off his bike and pushed it beside him, letting it fall to the ground near the entrance. He pressed his face to the window. No sign of life, just rows of bookshelves and haphazard stacks of paperbacks strewn across the counter.

Just then, he thought he saw a faint outline of a man behind the curtain of beads. He jiggled the door knob, surprised when the door opened, followed by the welcome chime.

"Hello," Lenny said, sticking his head through the open doorway.

He took a step inside. "Hello. Is anybody here?"

No answer. He closed the door behind him and crept past the counter.

"Mr. Porter? You there?"

Lenny moved closer to the back room separated by the curtain that looked like a flashback from the sixties. A funny image flashed through Lenny's mind of Mr. Porter dressed in a tie-dye t-shirt, polyester bell-bottom pants, and sporting a long, stringy beard.

That was his last thought before he crumpled to the floor, out cold from the sudden blow to his head.

Catch and Release

Dr. Hartman stared at the dark, empty bookstore through the windshield of Detective Sloan's squad car. "Doesn't look like anyone is here."

"You may be right, but we need to check it out anyway," Detective Sloan said.

The two got out of the car and walked to the entrance of the store. Sloan twisted the knob, but found it locked. He peered into the window. "Yep, looks like nobody's home." He turned to Dr. Hartman. "Come on. We might have a better chance of finding Porter at his apartment." They returned to the car.

As they drove away, Lenny, still unconscious, was being dragged along the storage room floor.

Plumes of dust filled the stale air within the abandoned church and invaded Ariel's sinuses, forcing her to sneeze and her eyes to water. She found an old tattered piece of cloth under one of the pews that she cleaned as best she could and used as a tissue. She thought if she didn't die from exposure, her allergies would surely kill her.

She smacked her parched lips. Her mouth felt like cotton and her throat gritty as sand. Ariel remembered reading an article that about twenty years ago, this church was refurbished by the Historical Society. But when the money dried up a few years later, so did the upkeep to the building, which was then boarded up and forgotten. Still, there was a chance that some modern conveniences were added, such as a water fountain.

Ariel knew that the likelihood water was still turned on to the chapel was slim, but she had to at least look. She ran her hand along the wall, feeling for anything that felt like a valve or faucet. As she walked, the wooden planks squeaked under her feet. Drawing nearer to the platform, she noticed the floorboards began to sag under her weight. She bounced up and down to test the floor's strength.

Crack! The board snapped. Ariel jumped backwards and fell onto her bottom, her foot trapped in the rotted planks. She stared at the splintered wood, surprised to see light coming up through the floor.

She quickly crawled to the hole and peered into its throat. The scent of dirt filled her nostrils. She thought she could see the ground. With both hands, she quickly tugged at the floorboards until she had made an opening wide enough for her to squeeze through.

Letting her feet dangle over the edge of the hole, she jumped onto the soft earth beneath. She closed her eyes for fear of coming face-to-face with bugs or spiders and wriggled out from underneath the chapel.

Dirty and covered in cobwebs, Ariel ran as fast as her feet could carry her—far away from the old church that entrapped her, past the granite monuments to the dead that littered the landscape … straight into the arms of a man who stepped from behind a tree.

"Hey, Sloan, you there?" said a voice through Detective Sloan's car radio.

He grabbed the mouthpiece. "Yeah, Bernice. Dr. Hartman and I are on our way to Porter's apartment. What's up?"

"That lady over at the library you talked to just called and said she figured out how to retrieve whatever it was that Ariel was looking at on the computer. But she's locking up and wants to know if it's important enough to stick around."

Detective Sloan slammed on the brakes and made a quick u-turn, hitting the curb on the other side of the road. "Tell her we're on our way."

Revelations

"Let me go! Let me go!" screamed Ariel, struggling to free herself from the stranger's grip. To her surprise, her captor released his hold.

"Whoa! I'm not going to hurt you. You can stop hitting me now," he said, hands raised in surrender.

When he pulled away, Ariel got a good look at the man. Her mouth hung open from the shock. "Mr. Porter. W-W-What are you doing here?" she stammered. Of all people to run into at night in a cemetery, it just had to be the one man she helped put in jail. But, here he stood, in the flesh, free as a bird. Fear coursed through Ariel's veins like rivers of ice. She took a careful step back, increasing the distance between her and the bookstore owner.

"Don't worry, Ariel. I'm not going to hurt you," he said soothingly.

She took another step, ready to run if she had to. "I asked what you were doing here, Mr. Porter."

He lowered his arms and stared off into space. "I'm here to visit Elizabeth's grave, if you must know. I just got out of jail and needed a place to think." He turned to Ariel. "After I lost the chest, thanks in part to you and that detective, I found myself completely at a loss about what to do next. I thought it would help to come back here—to where it all started."

"Where what started?" Ariel said.

"My roots. My quest." he replied. "Elizabeth Walker is my ancestor, as is her son Micah. For generations members of my family have believed that she left a fortune to him—the details of which were hidden somewhere in that diary, which has been handed down from father to son since the days of Micah. When my father passed away a few months ago, I inherited the book."

"So it *was* your family that held the diary in safe-keeping all this time? Does that make you the person who loaned the diary to the library?"

"Yes to both questions. Before I did, I discovered a secret compartment within the binding of the diary. After all, I inspect old books for a living. Inside, I found a skeleton key and a decoder that helped me decipher a hidden message in an exhaustive accounting of military armament and casualties that Louis wrote in the diary. What I thought was a bunch of mumbo-jumbo turned out to be a secret code to certain words in specific verses of Galatians that spelled out the directions to the chest's location."

"I know," said Ariel. "I saw the list of verses that Detective Sloan took from you when you were arrested. I can still remember it: *Bear fifteen with cross. Walk three and one past church. Stand measure three under*. It sounded like directions, but I still haven't figured out how it led to the trunk's hiding place."

"It told me to start at Elizabeth's grave and walk at a fifteen-degree angle thirty-one feet past the church where I was to dig three feet down." Mr. Porter sighed and then stared intently at Ariel. "I felt when I found the chest that I was so close to proving if there was a fortune or not."

"Does all of this treasure hunting have anything to do with the emeralds?"

A stunned expression came over Mr. Porter's face. "You saw inside the box?"

Ariel nodded.

He let his shoulders droop. "Then I suppose you already know if the legend is true or not, don't you?"

Ariel shook her head. "I don't. But I have a good idea who does. Come on. We've got to find a distant cousin of yours, quick."

The library parking lot was empty except for a dinged-up early model Toyota Corolla parked near the front. The inside of the library was pitch-black except for a few overhead lights kept lit for security reasons.

As Detective Sloan walked up to the entrance, he could see the librarian sitting at the Collection Counter, her eyes peering into a book she held near her face. The detective knocked on the glass door, jarring her.

She held up a finger, a sign to give her a minute. After she dug a set of keys from her purse, she quickly walked to the side door and unlocked it, pushing it open to let in Detective Sloan and Dr. Hartman.

"Thanks for coming," she said, relocking the tumblers. "When you left, I called Mrs. Thompson to let her know what was up. She showed me how to reinstate what Ariel pulled up on the computer. Follow me, and I will show you."

The librarian led them back to the Genealogy archives. A few keystrokes later, she motioned for the men to take a look.

Both Detective Sloan and Dr. Hartman bent down, studied the contents of the screen, and turned their heads slowly toward one another.

"May we have a copy of this?" Sloan asked the librarian.

She hit the Print button and left the room to retrieve the copy.

While she was gone, Detective Sloan turned back to Dr. Hartman, "Did you know that Dr. Smith was related to Louis Preston, the diary's author?"

"I had no idea." Dr. Hartman continued to stare into the computer screen.

Reaching for his walkie-talkie, Detective Sloan said, "I guess I better get an officer over to Dr. Smith's house to question him."

"I don't think it will do you any good."

The detective furrowed his brow. "And why is that?"

"Because he left for Central America." Dr. Hartman leaned against the cubicle wall, arms folded. "He came by my office early this afternoon saying he got a call from a group of archeologists who were just cleared by the government to investigate an ancient Mayan ruin they discovered, but had only a week to do it. They asked for his expertise and told him he had a ticket waiting for him at the airport if he could get away. He said to me that he had cleared his calendar, cancelled his classes, and was headed home to pack."

"When was this?"

Dr. Hartman shrugged. "About 11 AM, I guess."

Detective Sloan rubbed his eyes, more for thinking than out of fatigue. "That was about the time he left our office after deciphering all those documents in the box Porter found. He told us they were nothing more than old love letters and insignificant ramblings of a heart-sick woman longing for her husband to return from war." He drew out a long breath. "Now, I'm not so sure."

The detective yanked his walkie-talkie from his shoulder strap. "Bernice, this is Sloan. I need you to put out an APB for Dr. Allen Smith. Have an officer check the airports. He may have boarded a plane for Central America. Then get an officer over to his house."

"Got it," Bernice said. "Anything else?"

"Yeah, I may need a search warrant. Better call Judge Nelson."

Dr. Hartman's phone chirped. He flipped it open. "Hello," he said. His face grew darker as he listened to the caller. "Okay, I'll let Detective Sloan know. Don't worry. Just keep praying."

"What are you going to let me know?" Detective Sloan asked.

Dr. Hartman somberly returned his cell phone back to its case. "Lenny's missing. My wife went to check on him in his room, but he wasn't there. She's looked everywhere. His bike's gone. We don't …" He stopped, covered his face, and began to weep.

Detective Sloan put a hand on Dr. Hartman's shoulder. "We'll find him and Ariel, I promise."

The Cave

Lenny roused from an unconscious stupor, his head pounding like a drum during a rock concert. When he attempted to soothe his aching temples, he realized he could not move his arms. His hands were tied behind him and bound to a metal chair. Struggling to free himself, he found that his feet were strapped to the legs of the chair.

Dazed and disoriented, he scanned the room. Everything he saw was in double. He slowed his breathing trying to relax ... to think. "Where am I?" he said groggily.

, His vision soon returned to normal, and Lenny was able to study his surroundings. A single lightbulb hung over wooden stairs illuminating a dank, brick room. Old furniture and piles of newspapers and magazines lay cluttered under layers of dust and spider webs. Lenny was trapped in someone's basement. But whose? And where?

He focused his gaze toward the wall on the opposite side where he saw a huge gaping hole. Just inside, a lantern strung from a rope lit the entrance to what seemed to be a cave. Lenny strained to make out the substances within the rocks that glimmered in the lantern's rays like dancing starlight.

As his mind tried to make sense of what he was looking at, a shadow passed over the gleaming objects, turning them black. Soon, a man appeared holding a pick axe.

The man stepped into full view near the cave's opening and glared at Lenny. A grin passed across his lips at the sight of Lenny's frightened state.

"Ah, I see you're finally awake." He bounced the pick axe menacingly in his hands. "Whatever shall we do with you now, young man?"

Another night of clear skies and a bright moon helped Ariel and Mr. Porter maneuver through the maze of thick shrubs and tall trees in the wooded area beside the cemetery. Still, Mr. Porter did not have the energy that Ariel had.

"Wait, Ariel!"

Ariel turned back, realizing Mr. Porter had stopped. "Okay, but we need to hurry before it's too late."

Mr. Porter bent over, struggling to catch his breath. "Okay," he said, sucking in air. "Why don't we rest a minute and you tell me again why you suspect Dr. Smith." On the run, Ariel filled Mr. Porter in on how she discovered Dr. Smith's ancestry and her suspicions of him.

"It's simple," she said, rocking on her feet, anxious to return to the chase. "You're obviously not the thief because you own the diary. And Dr. Smith is not only related to the diary's author, but I'm pretty sure he lied."

"He lied? About what?" Mr. Porter said, stretching his legs.

"He said that he did not know anything about the diary. Yet, he's on the museum's Board of Directors. I saw of picture of him hanging on Mrs. Carmichael's wall. How can a member of the museum board not know anything about the most significant exhibit that has come to the museum?" She smiled to herself, remembering Detective Sloan's advice. "Besides, all great detectives know that to find the truth, you have to eliminate the lies."

Mr. Porter laughed. "You are a clever one."

"Maybe, but I still haven't figured out why you were at the museum the night of the crime. It was you that Chelsea saw, right?"

"Most likely. But the book she thought she saw under my arm was just my journal. I went to the museum to look at the old maps of Summerville against the one in the diary. Did you know they are almost identical, yet nothing like the maps of the Battle of Trenton?"

Ariel nodded. "Yep, it's of the graveyard."

Mr. Porter gave Ariel a knowing smile. "As I said, you are a clever one. Then have you figured out who Barnabus is—the person Louis dedicated the diary to?"

"Elizabeth's husband, I thought," Ariel replied.

"Nope," Mr. Porter said smiling. Ariel gave him a curious look. "It was Micah," he continued. "His real name was Barnabus Micah Walker. He was named after his father. But after Louis and Elizabeth died, people just referred to him as Micah. That really caused a lot of confusion later on about the diary."

"I guess so," Ariel said. "How are you feeling? You ready to go?"

"I think I've got my second wind. Let's go find this fiend, Dr. Smith."

Ariel turned to run, plowing right into something solid behind the bushes in the path.

"Umph!" she groaned as she fell on her back.

Mr. Porter raced to help her to her feet. "Are you all right?"

"I think so, but I feel like I just ran into a bus."

Pulling away the limbs and debris, Mr. Porter turned back to Ariel. "Pretty close. It's a car. Someone deliberately tried to hide it from view. But why?"

Ariel pointed to Porter's Bookstore nearby. "Looks like whoever it was parked it close by your shop."

"I didn't know we had come this far." He looked down at Ariel. "Are you okay? Can you still do a little more sleuthing?"

"You bet I can." She pushed herself up from the ground.

"Good. I got an idea to catch us a thief."

Too Close for Comfort

Ariel crept into Porter's Bookstore through the back door, a step behind Mr. Porter. She glanced over the bookstore's darkened storage room. She could just make out the outlines of several boxes piled high and long tables used for sorting books.

Mr. Porter stopped just inside and put a finger over his lips, a gesture for Ariel not to make a sound. He then went to the alarm box on the wall. "Just as I suspected. It's off." He hit a button on the keypad.

"Doesn't look like anybody is back here or in the store," he whispered. Motioning to the shaft of light coming through the floorboards, he said, "But someone's here, no doubt."

Waving for Ariel to follow, he moved quietly to a trap door on the floor. Gently, he raised the heavy lid, pausing each time it made a squeak. Ariel leaned over his shoulder and watched as the opening widened to reveal a set of wooden stairs that led to the basement. Slowly, Mr. Porter and Ariel began to descend the steps.

Halfway down, they heard noises coming from below. Mr. Porter and Ariel froze mid-stride. Ariel turned an ear toward the sounds and listened.

Voices!

But not just any voice—it was Lenny's!

Ariel sprinted down the stairs after her brother.

Mr. Porter reached for Ariel as she ran past him, missing her arm by a fraction of an inch.

Detective Sloan was pleased when Officer Frazier handed him the stolen diary, which he found in Dr. Smith's home office tucked neatly in a drawer. "Yep, took some arm-twisting to get Judge Nelson to sign off on that warrant with the scant evidence I had, but it paid off, I see."

Officer Frazier just nodded and walked away to continue the search of the home.

Another policeman stepped next to Detective Sloan and handed him a pair of black gloves. "I found these, Detective. Should I bag 'em?"

Sloan laughed out loud when he noticed the snag on the index finger of the left glove. He nudged Dr. Hartman who looked on beside him. "Your daughter found a black thread wedged into the display case that I and the other officers overlooked. And here we have the glove that probably matches that thread, along with Dr. Smith's DNA most likely inside them." He handed the pair back to the officer. "Bag them," he said.

"This is all well and good, but we are no closer to finding my children," Dr. Hartman said remorsefully.

Before Detective Sloan had time to respond, Officer Frazier called to him from the next room. "Hey Sloan. Got a call that a silent alarm just sounded at Porter's Bookstore. You want me to send a unit over to check it out?"

In less than a minute, Detective Sloan and Dr. Hartman were racing down the sleepy streets of Summerville, lights flashing.

Lenny gazed in shock as he watched Ariel run into the room. "No, Ariel! Get out of here!"

Ariel froze at the sight of Lenny strapped to the chair. Her eyes darted to the figure that emerged from the cavernous hole in the wall.

"Ah, what a pleasure that your nosy sister could join you, Leonard," said Dr. Smith, still gripping the pick axe in his hand.

"Let him go!" hollered Ariel.

Dr. Smith drew his head back and laughed. "I'm afraid I can't do that, young lady. You would have been better off to have stayed in the old church where I left you. But no! You could not heed my warning. Did my phone call not make you think twice about your insistent meddling? And then your brother had to play hero and come looking for you. Now, you both must be severely dealt with, I'm afraid."

He took a step closer to Ariel. She glanced at her brother pinned and helpless. Then she turned back, expecting Mr. Porter to come racing down the stairs after her. Where did he go? She hoped to get help.

Ariel had to buy some time. "Wait! At least tell me what you found. You know, like you said I'm nosy." She forced a smile.

"Very well," Dr. Smith said. "I guess that's the least I can do since it was you who suggested to the police that I look at the contents of the chest. If not for you, I might never have guessed the whereabouts to this vast cache of precious stones."

Ariel could have kicked herself for suggesting to Detective Sloan that he have Dr. Smith translate those documents. At the time, though, she had no reason to suspect him. If she could go back in time, knowing what she knew now, she'd certainly never mention his name. Then again, if she knew then what she knew now, this guy would already be behind bars.

Dr. Smith leaned the pick axe against the wall. "Elizabeth's journal hidden in that chest Mr. Porter pulled from the ground revealed a secret cave under her house given to her by the Indians upon settling in Summerville." He waved a hand loosely in the air. "Apparently, she helped deliver the chief's baby. If she didn't, it would likely have died along with his wife during labor. In gratitude, he offered her land that included a mine rich in emeralds—the same land that she built her homestead on."

"But how did you know to look here?"

Dr. Smith snickered. "Because, anyone who knows anything about Summerville's history knows that this store stands in the same location where her house once stood. What no one knew, however, was that there was a vein of emerald ore that ran underneath, which she concealed behind that wall. You see, this was not always a basement. It used to be the root cellar to her home. Unfortunately for her, she died from complications after giving birth to her son, Micah, before she could enjoy it. Of course, Micah's father died in war just a few days before he was born. Such a tragedy, don't you think?"

Ariel could not help but see the irony in Elizabeth's situation. After she saved the chief's wife during labor, she would die following her own. Dr. Smith helped explain why Elizabeth's and Barnabus' dates of death were so close to Micah's birthday.

"She lived long enough to tell one soul about her secret: my long-lost ancestor, Louis," continued Dr. Smith, "who valiantly pledged to keep the secret until Micah was of age to be told—the details of which he hid in cryptic messages inside that diary of lies. Too bad the old fool died before he had a chance to tell the brat what they meant."

"But how did you steal the diary when Mrs. Carmichael had the only key?" Ariel said.

He gave a wry smile. "Ah, that was a clever ploy on my part, I must confess. When that old windbag opened the case for me to examine the book that night, I distracted her long enough to wedge a piece of paper in the latch. When she closed the lid, she didn't even check to see if it re-locked. I then slipped into the storage room and hid until she went into her office, like she does every night. When all was quiet, I crept out, snatched the diary from the case and went out the side door."

Overhead, the sound of running footsteps echoed throughout the basement. Dr. Smith hurried into the cave. He grabbed a duffle bag that bulged at the seams under a heavy weight.

Ariel ran over to the cave's opening where she saw Dr. Smith scale a ladder with one hand clutching the bag. Behind her, the stairs groaned and creaked under the strain of marching feet. She turned to see Detective Sloan leading the charge, gun drawn, followed by another armed officer. Behind them ran Mr. Porter and her father.

"He went that way. Up that ladder," Ariel said, pointing.

Detective Sloan reached the ladder just as the thieving professor's feet cleared the last rung and disappeared on the surface. The detective quickly climbed after him.

The other officer sprinted back up the stairs to take up the flank.

The room grew eerily quiet, everyone frozen and unsure of what to do next. Lenny broke the silence. "Anybody want to help me out of this chair?"

Ariel raced over to her brother. She threw her arms around him. "I'm so sorry to have gotten you into this mess, Lenny."

"It's not your fault, little sis. I should have been there for you. I'm sorry too. I shouldn't have been so hard on you."

Dr. Hartman went over to Ariel and Lenny and pulled them close. "I'm just so glad you both are okay."

"Me too, Dad," said Lenny. Then he looked down at his trapped feet. "Now, if it's not too much trouble, can someone untie me?"

Ariel tugged on the rope that held his legs. Dr. Hartman peeled away the tape to loosen Lenny's hands. Soon free, Lenny stood on shaky legs and rubbed his sore wrists. "Thanks. I thought I was a goner there for a minute."

A somber look fell on Dr. Hartman's face. "I too was worried that you both might have been goners." He again wrapped both Ariel and Lenny tightly in his arms. The two gasped for air between laughs.

Mr. Porter stood to the side and watched, smiling. "All's well that ends well, I guess," he said.

Ariel looked at her brother. "So how did you get trapped down here?"

"I came here looking for you. I found the door unlocked, so I came inside. Next thing I know I was out like a light. What about you?"

Ariel shared her experience of getting knocked out too at the library and being taken to the old cemetery chapel. She described how she escaped and ran into Mr. Porter.

Dr. Hartman patted Mr. Porter on the back. "I'm really glad you were around. If you had not set off that silent alarm, no telling what might have happened."

Mr. Porter nodded toward the cave. "I'm just sorry that Dr. Smith got away."

"Not so fast," came a voice from the stairwell. Everyone turned to see Detective Sloan dragging a heavy duffle bag down the steps. At the bottom, he flung it onto the floor at Mr. Porter's feet. The detective bent down and unzipped it. "Mr. Porter, I believe these belong to you," he said, pulling out a handful of greenish stones.

Mr. Porter stared in amazement. He began to speak, but had difficulty forming the words to say. Ariel walked over to the bookstore owner and put an arm around him, beaming with joy alongside her new friend.

Can't Judge a Book
by Its Cover

A couple of days later, things had begun to return to normal. Lenny went with his father to collect his bike, which was found tossed into the field behind the bookstore. Mrs. Hartman left for the grocery store. Ariel sat alone at the kitchen table scanning the *Summerville Times* in search of a new case to solve. What she saw filled her with surprise … and happiness.

On the front page was a big black-and-white photograph of Mr. Porter shaking the mayor's hand. The headline read, "Local Bookstore Owner Donates Millions to Schools and Museums." The article went on to describe Mr. Porter's relation to the son of one of the town's founders who was orphaned as an infant. Unbeknownst to the child because of the death of his uncle, he had become the sole heir to an emerald mine on his mother's homestead. The property then passed down in Mr. Porter's family (along with the diary), which was later turned into the bookstore.

When asked the reason for such generosity, Mr. Porter was quoted as saying, "Elizabeth's life was built on selflessness and giving. It's proven by the sacrifice she and her brother made to establish Summerville and by her dying wish that her son have a good start in life. I think she would be proud that after all these years Summerville has prospered and will continue to prosper through this inheritance."

Ariel sighed a happy sigh. Everyone so easily chalked up poor Mr. Porter as the thief, including Ariel for a time. But if she had not kept searching for the truth, Dr. Smith would certainly have gotten away with the loot.

A knock on the door stirred Ariel from her thoughts. She opened it to a delivery man dressed in a blue and orange uniform. "Package for Miss Ariel Hartman," the man announced.

"That's me," said Ariel. After she signed the delivery man's log sheet, he handed her a shoe-sized box wrapped in brown paper.

She closed the door and carried the package to the table. After she ripped into it, she reached inside and pulled out a letter.

Dear Ariel,

I want to thank you for solving this case and clearing my name. Do you remember me telling you that the dedication in the diary was really for Micah? Well, I think I finally realize what the actual message meant: "May you find the treasure within that makest thy heart rich." Louis not only wanted him to find the emeralds, but a treasure that could change his heart. I've been reading Elizabeth's Bible, and I'm pretty sure he was talking about Christ. Why else would Louis use Scriptures to mark the steps to Elizabeth's buried trunk? Pray for me. In the meantime, please accept these as tokens of my gratitude.

Your friend,
Nate Porter

Ariel peeled away the tissue inside the box. She found a copy of the book *To Catch a Thief* that she admired when she first visited Mr. Porter at his shop. When she pulled it out, something fell to the floor. She looked down to find a dark green, shimmering object lying at her feet. Ariel recognized an uncut emerald when she saw one, but she stood locked in place, mouth agape, staring at the beautiful rock in disbelief.

As she bent down to grasp the emerald in her shaking hand, the telephone rang. Ariel stuck the stone in her pocket and raced to the phone, checking the Caller ID before she picked up the receiver. It was Chelsea!

"Hello," Ariel answered hesitantly.

"Hi, Ariel. It's Chelsea," said the perky voice on the other end. "So sorry I didn't call you back. My dad's aunt died and we had to go to her funeral. And with all that was going on back here with the theft, Mom and Dad decided we should make a family trip out of it and stay over some."

Ariel was relieved to know that Chelsea was not avoiding her.

"Oh that's all right," Ariel said. "Lots of things have happened."

"I know. My mom read me the article in the paper. You want to come over and tell me all about it? I live at 2323 Sycamore."

"That's just down the road. Give me fifteen minutes?"

Chelsea lived in a two-story red brick house with a wrap-around porch and large gable windows extending from a gray-shingled roof. The numbers 2323 were painted white in block lettering on the side of the curb.

Ariel parked her bike in the driveway next to a light blue minivan. She slowly approached the front door, admiring its intricate etched glass and dark stained wood. Both of Chelsea's parents were attorneys and could afford a nice house.

She pushed the doorbell and a high pitched *ding-dong* chimed. An eternity seemed to pass before a tall woman with striking blue eyes and long blond hair opened the door. She wore a sleeveless white silk blouse and a light gray pen-striped skirt that highlighted her trim frame.

"Hold on just a sec," the lady said into the telephone she held up to her ear. She covered the mouthpiece with her hand. "Can I help you?"

"Is Chelsea at home?" Ariel replied.

"Oh, you must be Ashley or Amanda, or something like that. Chelsea said she might have a friend drop by."

"It's Ariel," Ariel corrected.

"Oh, right. Sorry. I'm Chelsea's mom. Come in." She stepped aside to let Ariel pass. Ariel walked into an elaborate foyer that flowed into a curved stairway. A ten-foot crystal chandelier hung overhead accenting the gold-gilded furniture that decorated the entryway. "Chelsea's in her bedroom right now. You wait here while I go get her." Chelsea's mother sauntered up the stairs and disappeared beyond the second story balcony.

Ariel let her eyes roam across the entry of the home into the lush dining room off to the side. Just then, Chelsea bounced down the stairs dressed in a pink sun dress.

She gave Ariel a warm smile. "Thanks for coming," Chelsea said. "Let's go to my room and talk." She escorted Ariel up the stairs and past a large den area littered with coloring books, crayons, and dolls. "Sorry for the mess. My little sister and her friends destroy the place. But then my room isn't much better."

They walked down a hallway and into a brightly colored room with large sunflowers and daisies painted on the walls. Ariel noticed the walls matched Chelsea's bedspread. "You like flowers, huh?"

"Yeah. My dad painted the room. He copied the flowers from my comforter, as you can probably tell. They're okay, but I like kittens better. Dad couldn't paint kittens."

Ariel sat at the corner of the bed. "It's very nice. In fact, your whole house is really nice."

Taking the chair at her desk, Chelsea said, "Thanks. So tell me about the case. The paper didn't say much about the actual crime, only that a professor at the college was arrested." She wrinkled her brow. "Hey, isn't your dad a professor?"

"Yes, but it wasn't him. It was a guy named Dr. Allen Smith," Ariel went on to recount the events of the week. Ariel told her how both Mr. Porter and Dr. Smith were descendants of the families that were connected to the diary. She described the emerald mine underneath Mr. Porter's bookstore and how she and her brother had been kidnapped by Dr. Smith.

Chelsea sat amazed as she listened to Ariel. "So what helped you figure out that Mr. Porter and Dr. Smith were related?"

"Do you remember when we had that assignment to trace our family tree?"

Chelsea nodded slightly. "Yeah, vaguely. I have to admit, I'm not the brainiac like you."

"I don't know about that," Ariel said, laughing. "Anyway, I used what I learned in that project to trace Louis Preston and Elizabeth Walker's family. Elizabeth's was pretty easy. It led straight to Porter. Louis' was a little more difficult."

"How so?"

"I got as far as an Orville and Henry Smythe and got stuck. Then I remembered this picture of a blacksmith, but the caption had it spelled B-L-A-C-K-S-M-Y-T-H-E. That had me thinking that some people named Smythe later changed the spelling to Smith. After I got that, it didn't take long for Dr. Smith's name to pop up."

"Wow! That's pretty impressive," Chelsea said.

Ariel stared up at the ceiling. "Yeah, if only I can have the same luck figuring out what happened to that attorney person that sent the diary to the museum in the first place." She shrugged then added, "I guess I'll go ask Mr. Porter one day."

"Actually, I may know the answer to that one."

"You do?" Ariel asked, surprised.

"Yeah, my Mom found him in her lawyer database. It was some kid straight out of college who just passed the bar exam. He opened a small practice. Then, all of the sudden, he closed it down and went to work for a big law firm in New York. I bet Mr. Porter was his first, and probably only, client."

"That sounds like Mr. Porter—big heart to give a kid a chance like that."

"Yeah, I just wish the school had a big heart and would give us another week off. This one was just a little too exciting for me."

As Chelsea talked about how bummed out she was that Spring Break was drawing to a close, Ariel reflected on how perceptions changed between Dr. Smith and Mr. Porter in one short week. A well respected professor turned out to be nothing more than a thief and kidnapper driven by greed while the mysterious newcomer with a penchant for late-night strolls in dark alleys and digs in the graveyard was actually the good guy. That old saying, "you can't judge a book by its cover," certainly rang true for those two … and for a nearly two hundred and fifty year-old diary.

Epilogue

Two weeks later...

The man, decked in a pen-striped suit, walked into the police station, briefcase in hand. He flashed his business card to the officer at the front desk. "I'm here to see Dr. Allen Smith," he said.

The policeman barely glanced over the card. "He expecting you?"

"I don't think so, but I'm sure he'll want to see me."

The visitor did not have long to wait. Within a few minutes, he was ushered into a small room with a single table and two chairs, one of which was occupied by Dr. Smith, clad in an orange jumper, the words "County Jail" printed on the back.

"Dr. Smith, my name is Arthur Ridgeway," the man said, taking the empty chair. "I'm the attorney who represented Mr. Nathaniel Porter in the loan of his diary to the museum."

Dr. Smith nodded smugly. "Yeah? What can I do for you?"

From his briefcase, Mr. Ridgeway grabbed a stack of papers and a yellow notepad. "I've been retained by Mr. Porter to represent you in your legal proceedings, if you should so choose to hire me."

The imprisoned professor gave a slight chuckle. "Let me get this straight: Porter wants you to be my lawyer? Aren't you a little young?"

"I was top of my class and practically aced the bar exam." Mr. Ridgeway handed him a pamphlet. "I will also have at my disposal some of the best minds in law who happen to work in the firm where I'm employed: Turner, Carter, and Boyd."

Dr. Smith slowly thumbed through the brochure. "Why is Porter doing this? I don't understand. I stole his diary."

Mr. Ridgeway leaned back in his seat. "Apparently, Mr. Porter has recently become a Christian. Having converted, he wants to extend his hand to you to help in every way. He told me that you should have the very best representation. You'll get that with me. And Mr. Porter is prepared to pay for all legal expenses."

Dr. Smith sat dazed until a smile swept across his face. "Mr. Ridgeway, I'm at a loss for words. This has got to be the kindest thing anyone has ever done for me. If being a Christian had this effect on Porter, maybe I should look into becoming one myself."

"That reminds me." Mr. Ridgeway reached back into his case and pulled out Elizabeth Walker's Bible, the one found in the trunk. "I've been asked to give this to you. Perhaps this will help you in your decision in becoming a Christian yourself."

Ariel's After "Word"

Wow! Imagine someone leaving you an emerald mine for your inheritance. That would be cool. It's also pretty interesting that Louis used verses from Galatians as clues that eventually lead to the discovery of the treasure. Why? Because there's a lot of similarities between this story and what Paul wrote about in the Epistle of Galatians.

During Paul's time, many believed that you had to follow the Law's customs to obtain a heavenly inheritance (the Law is what God gave Moses for the children of Israel after they left Egypt). In fact, there were false teachers that rose up in the church at Galatia who told born-again believers they weren't really saved unless they continued to practice some of these traditions. Paul called these teachers imposters. He taught that the Law was needed for a time until a special descendant of Abraham came along and paid the ultimate price for our salvation. We know who that is, right? Jesus.

Now it's your turn to play detective. Read Galatians and compare it with *The Diary Dilemma*. Can you find the similarities? Here are a few "hints" to guide you on your quest.

- Because of Dr. Smith's occupation (professor of history), he was an authority on history. But he was also a thief and a kidnapper. You could say he was an imposter because he pretended to be one thing but lived another way. Paul talks about imposters who claimed to be authorities on the Gospel, but who actually deceived people (Galatians 1:6-9).

- Dr. Smith was not the only expert in the story. Nate Porter was too because he understood about old, rare books and the history around them. Paul was the rightful expert on the Gospel to the saints at Galatia because he was the first to bring the Gospel to them, and he was trained by God Himself (Galatians 1:10-2:21).

- There was a long time that passed before Nate Porter unlocked Elizabeth Preston's secret of the treasure. It was a long time before God's promise to Abraham was fulfilled that all nations were to be blessed through him (Genesis 12:1-3). Paul says that the faithful are all children of Abraham with rights to God's promises (Galatians 3:1-25).

- Nate Porter was a direct descendant of Elizabeth Preston's son, Micah. Because of that, he was the rightful heir to the diary and the treasure. By God's son Jesus, we can all be children of God and have, as our inheritance, Heaven (Galatians 3:26-4:7).

- The story told of two families that knew there was some special secret the diary held, but only one of the families had true claim to the treasure: the family of Elizabeth's son, Micah. Paul explained that Abraham had two sons: one from a slave woman (named Hagar) and another from a free woman (Abraham's wife Sarah). Paul likened the son of the slave woman to the Law, which kept people in slavery for following traditions and depending on man. But the son of the free woman he likened to living by faith and trusting in Jesus, the Son of God (Galatians 4:8-31).

- Nate Porter's family protected the diary and kept it in perfect condition. We are to protect this Gospel and keep it just the way Christ originally intended it to be. We are not to return to our old sinful ways (Galatians 5:1-12).

- Dr. Smith envied Nate Porter for inheriting the diary and the secret treasure. That envy caused him to commit the crimes he did. Envy is just one of the many sins Paul mentioned that can keep us from inheriting the kingdom of God. Of course, Paul told us that we can let the Spirit of God lead us and we'll have the fruits of the Spirit (Galatians 5:13-26).

- Ariel did a good thing for Mr. Porter by pressing for the truth, which eventually proved his innocence. Mr. Porter did a good thing by letting the city of Summerville have some of the proceeds from the emerald mine to benefit the museum and the schools. These were selfless acts. Paul says that when we have an opportunity to do good for another, we are to do it (Galatians 6:1-18).